The Gold Flower Locket

The Dreary Portent

Megon Lashley

Published by Megon Lashley, 2024.

THE GOLD FLOWER LOCKET

First edition. April 26, 2024.

ISBN: 979-8224702664

Written by Megon Lashley.

Also by Megon Lashley

The Dreary Portent
The Window In The Painting
The Gold Flower Locket

Table of Contents

To my mom, Celest

CHAPTER ONE
A Locket On Display

A thick fog rose up from the damp cobblestones along the street. The milky haze billowed and twisted through the paths and alleyways, obscuring the buildings and shop signs all along the way. Hiding every storefront from sight.

All but one.

A little curiosity shop sat amongst the mist, unbothered by its gloom. Untouched by the dense fog. It was an odd little store, filled with unusual items. The light inside the shop was dim. Nothing more than a gentle amber glow from the lanterns strewn about the shelves. And the smell of cloves and spice filled the air in wafts of scented smoke.

The shopkeeper moved through the shadows of the store. Inky black hair fell across her impossibly pale skin. A flash of amber filled her eyes as she struck a match and lit the final lantern. Its wick burst into brightness with a soft sizzle. The back of the store illuminated, revealing the items on the surrounding shelves.

A beautiful antique ink pot and matching feather quill sat on a small writing table. An ordinary-looking photo album bound closed with a heavy padlock was sitting on a high shelf. A worn, patchy teddy bear was perched on the edge of an old wooden chair.

"Everything in this shop has a story," the woman began. "Each item has a past owner... and a future owner," she added with a smile. "Witches, widows, ghosts. They all leave a small piece of their past on the object. A small piece of *themselves*."

She slid her hands over a newly illuminated display as she walked toward the counter. The black velvet box in front of her held a single piece of jewelry. A necklace waiting for a new home.

The gold locket gleamed within the soft fabric lining of the box where it hung. A flower engraving bloomed gracefully across the front, beckoning to be worn. It glinted and beamed as the light danced upon its polished surface, shining delicately onto the flower etching.

The woman glanced at the locket, a wry smile playing at her lips. "This is one of our most elegant pieces. It really does have quite a story."

She pulled a book from a nearby shelf. It was bound in black leather with a picture of a gold locket embossed on the front. The pages within were filled with pictures and hand-written notes, all tucked neatly between the ink-filled leaflets. She flipped through the tome until she'd nearly reached the end and stopped.

"Ah, here we are." She smiled broadly. "This tale is a love story."

CHAPTER TWO
Jonas

Jonas Decker was an uncomplicated sort of man. He ran a small pub in the middle of town. Knew the names and orders of all his regulars. He even lived in a little room behind the bar. It was a simple existence that didn't afford him much opportunity for a personal life. Something that never bothered him; until *she* moved in across the street.

It was one week earlier when he first caught sight of her through his window. She was rolling a large trunk across the cobblestones and into the two story building just kitty-corner to his own. He watched her fumble with her new key. Her dark brown tresses loosely tangled into a long braid hanging over one shoulder. A few free tendrils curled gently and framed her face.

Sally Lockley.

She was a vision. A breath of fresh air in a town that had long since grown stale. And Jonas had made it his mission to see her each day since their first introduction. He popped in to visit with her whenever he had a slow moment at the pub. He'd never had much of a green thumb himself, but after a week of frequent visits, he'd grown to like her little plant shop.

Jonas peered through the square glass panes of the door, catching a glimpse of his own reflection in the glass. He quickly fussed with his unruly ginger locks. They never stayed where he put them. He pushed his hat back down over his hair and looked through the pane again, looking past his own image and into the little shop on the other side.

There she was. Sweet, beautiful Sally. She was watering a sickly-looking plant, and looking as lovely as ever. She spotted him and smiled, beckoning him in. Her smile shone with warmth and kindness.

He opened the door and stepped inside the shop. The storefront was warm and humid, a stark contrast to the chilly air outside. A sweet, earthy smell hit his senses the moment he walked in. Many of the plants were in full bloom, despite it being the dead of winter. "I didn't want to bother you if you weren't ready for visitors."

"Don't be silly. I've always got time for you, Mr. Decker."

"Please, call me Jonas."

Sally blushed and nodded. "Of course."

"So what is it you're working on there?" He pointed to the sickly-looking plant she held in her hands.

"Oh, this little plant has been feeling a bit under the weather since we moved in. I'd hoped it would perk up on its own, but I think it may need something extra." She walked behind the counter and pulled up a large metal canister. The scoop she used scraped loudly across the bottom of the can. She pulled it out, revealing a small amount of white powder.

Sally frowned at the meager amount. "It's a special plant food," she explained as she sprinkled it in the flowerpot. "It's so hard to come by and I have very little of it left. But it should be just the trick to get this little fella back on his feet." She smiled fondly at the wilted plant.

Jonas wasn't certain what kind of plant it was, but even ill, it looked dangerous. Spiked barbs covered its vines. Sharp, teeth-like edges surrounded the drooping red flowers. Jonas would have been more alarmed by its appearance, but everything in Sally's shop looked a *bit* dangerous. She specialized in exotic plants, most of which were carnivorous.

Despite the odd nature of her plants, the shop was lovely. The shelves and tables were lined with all sorts of unfamiliar looking flora. Vines and blossoms wound their way along the counters. Large blooms of color were everywhere, while bursts of fragrant scents filled the air.

And Sally was a vast improvement over the previous tenant. A foul tempered, foul smelling fishmonger named Lazlo. The shop was dreadful when he had it. He took no care in how he ran it, or the quality of his wares. The place always reeked of guts and fish parts he'd left to rot on the floor. The odor billowed through the streets.

Lazlo was a brute of a man. Unkempt and unreasonable. He complained about everything, started fights with every neighbor, and constantly cheated and gouged his customers. It was no surprise to anyone to see his building empty one morning. Rumor had it Lazlo may have accrued some lofty gambling debts in town, so he closed up shop in the dead of night and disappeared.

As far as Jonas was concerned, it was good riddance. He couldn't imagine Lazlo would be missed by anyone else on their street either. Sally, on the other hand, was a delight. The man who owned the pottery shop next door gifted her several colorful flower pots when she first moved in, which now had all manner of plants in them. Maeve, the woman who owned the bakery down the street, brought Sally a welcome basket of breads and pastries; she, in particular, was pleased to no longer have the smell of rotting fish in the neighborhood.

Everyone was charmed by Sally. Though some were a little too charmed for Jonas' liking. The bell above the shop door rang as a dashing, well-dressed man entered the shop. He wore a custom suit, perfectly shined leather shoes, and a bowler hat that alone probably cost more than Jonas' entire outfit. Jonas found himself suddenly tugging at his own secondhand waistcoat, uncomfortable and self conscious. The man smiled at the sight of Sally, and her eyes lit up as he entered.

"Dr. Miller!" she exclaimed. Jonas' stomach gave a small lurch at the delight in her voice.

"Sally, my dear! How are you?"

"Quite well, and you?"

"Better now that I've seen your face." Dr. Miller took her hand in his and kissed it gently.

Sally blushed.

Jonas could feel the blood rushing to his face.

"You alright, Decker? You look a bit flushed?" Dr. Miller asked with a wink toward Jonas. They'd been competing for Sally's attention all week. It seemed Miller thought he'd won.

Dr. Jefferson Miller; perfect and pressed. Not a blond hair out of place. He was handsome, rich, refined. Not to mention snide, condescending, arrogant... At least, that's how Jonas saw him. But no one else seemed to see it. They'd known each other since they were children, but they'd never been friends. Miller always had all the advantages; in school, in life, in love. It drove Jonas mad.

Jealousy had always been Jonas' worst flaw. He knew it; he tried to fight it, but it always made its way to the surface. So many past relationships tarnished and ruined because of it; but not this time. He was determined. Still, when he realized Miller also had designs on Sally, he could feel it bubbling inside him. How could he compete with such a man? A fancy school, a well-paying career, respected by the entire community.

Jonas watched spitefully as Sally and Miller talked and laughed. He nodded and smiled each time one of them looked his way, but in truth he'd stopped listening, more lost in his own thoughts than whatever charming story Miller was filling her head with. He forced himself to focus, to fight each petty thought that pushed its way to the front of his mind.

"Oh, you should see it in the spring, Sally," Miller said with a wide smile. "The flowers fill the entire garden square. You will love it."

"It sounds lovely. I can't wait." She turned to Jonas. "You didn't tell me the town planted such an elaborate garden in the square every spring. We should add some to it next year," she said excitedly.

Jonas smiled. "That sounds like a great idea."

"Would you help me arrange it?" she asked, still staring at Jonas.

He stared back, lost in the color of her eyes. So green they rivaled the leaves of every plant in her shop.

"Oh, Sally, we shouldn't put Decker out like that," Miller interrupted. "Poor ol' chap has a hard enough time keeping that dingy little dive afloat. We can't ask him to take time away from it."

He wanted to be angry at the insult, but Miller was right. What life could Jonas offer Sally? On a barman's take from a pub barely staying above water? Sally had every reason in the world to favor Miller, to be a wealthy doctor's wife one day. And yet, whenever the three of them were in the same company, it was on Jonas where her eyes lingered the longest. Maybe there was some hope there after all.

Sally smiled sympathetically. "I certainly understand. I have a bit of trouble sometimes as well. Not everyone appreciates my plants the way I-" Sally's gaze lingered at the window. Her smile fell. Her brow furrowed.

Jonas turned to look; an older gentleman was ducking into an alley across the street. A frail-looking body tucked into an expensive suit, scraggly gray hair popping out from beneath his hat. Jonas didn't recognize him; but he was gone so quickly, it was hard to be certain. It didn't seem all that suspicious, but Sally's eyes were still fixed on where he'd stood.

"Sally? Are you alright?" Jonas asked.

She pulled her gaze from the window and smiled hesitantly at him. "Yes, of course." She shook her head and composed herself. "I just... I thought I saw someone I used to know." She looked around the shop, still seeming uneasy. "Well, I really must get back to tending my plants." She smiled. "It's been so lovely visiting with both of you." With that, she quickly bustled away and disappeared into the room behind the counter.

CHAPTER THREE
A Shadowy Figure

Jonas headed back into the chilly air and started across the street toward the pub, but stopped abruptly as the sound of his own name drew his attention.

"Jonas! Jonas!" a sweet voice cut through the cold morning air.

He turned to see an attractive, well-dressed woman walking briskly toward him. "I'm glad I caught you," she smiled breathlessly as she reached him.

"Clara?" Jonas smiled. "What are you doing out here in the cold? Shouldn't you be in the office?" Clara Sable was Miller's nurse. She was a pleasant looking, kind natured young woman. Dusty blond hair, tied tightly in a bun. Large, dark eyes. And a smile that held a tremendous amount of compassion.

"I'm looking for Dr. Miller. A patient needs him right away. Have you seen him this morning?"

Jonas nodded and looked back at Sally's shop, just as the door swung open and Miller stepped out onto the sidewalk. He was absentmindedly slipping on a pair of expensive Italian leather gloves. He didn't even seem to notice Clara at first.

"Jefferson Miller!" Clara said sternly. "What on earth are you doing?"

Miller looked surprised and a little confused.

"You were supposed to pick up the prescriptions and bring them straight back to the office. You have patients waiting on them."

Miller furrowed his brow. "Right." He patted the breast of his coat. "I have them right here. I just…" He looked back towards Sally's shop and shrugged. "Honestly, I don't know what I was thinking."

Clara sighed and smiled at Jonas. "Thank you. Always lovely to see you, Jonas."

Jonas nodded and crossed the street toward his pub. Behind him, he could hear Clara and Miller bickering as they headed down the street. Jonas smiled to himself as he overheard her chastise him for *gallivanting around when he should be tending to patients.*

"What has gotten into you lately?" Clara huffed. "A *plant store?*"

"It seemed like a good idea at the time," he heard Miller argue.

Their voices faded into the distance as they made their way toward Miller's office, and Jonas had crossed the street to his pub.

As Jonas reached the door, he saw an elderly, white-haired man sitting outside, bundled in a tattered coat and propped against the pub wall.

"What are you doing here, Abner?"

Abner opened his eyes halfway and stared up at Jonas. "You open yet?"

Jonas rolled his eyes. "Have you been out here all night?"

Abner shrugged. "It was a late one last night. Easier to just curl up on the street than trudge all the way home." He stood up and attempted to straighten the rumpled clothes beneath his coat.

"It's not safe for you to sleep out here," Jonas argued, opening the door and letting Abner in the pub. Jonas took off his coat and hat as Abner sat himself down at the bar. "I hope you know I'm not serving alcohol this early?"

"Oh, that's no problem. I'll just have some of that lovely coffee you brew."

Jonas poured the coffee into a mug. Steam rolled up from the surface as he placed it on the bar. Abner took it happily, then produced a monogrammed flask from inside his coat pocket and tipped it into the coffee.

Jonas sighed and shook his head. He felt a little silly for not having seen that coming.

"So, I saw you skipping off to see your lady friend across the street this morning," Abner said, taking a long sip from the mug. "How are things going there?"

Jonas shrugged. "Well enough, I suppose..."

"Also saw Dr. Miller heading in there," Abner smiled and raised one of his stark white eyebrows.

"Drink your coffee," Jonas huffed.

Abner let out a small laugh. "Oh, don't worry about the doctor. You're just as good a man as him. Maybe not when it comes to money, or success, or looks, or-"

"Thanks, Abner," he interrupted. "Any more of your pep talk and I might not find the will to get out of bed in the morning."

"Oh, you know what I mean."

Jonas smiled. "I do." Abner meant well, Jonas knew that. They'd been friends for years.

"Besides, it's not the doctor I'd be worried about if I were you."

Jonas furrowed his brow. "What do you mean?"

"Was nodding off in the alley last night and I saw him... a man sneaking around in the dark outside Miss Sally's shop. Not sure if he was sneaking out or sneaking in. But it was awful late for respectable company, if you get my meaning."

"Who was it?" Jonas asked.

"Didn't get a good look. Stuck to the shadows, he did. I suspect he didn't want to be spotted." Abner raised an eyebrow. "Might be a married sort of man. Though you didn't hear that from me. Wouldn't want to start a neighborhood scandal."

"Do you remember anything about him?"

Abner shook his head. "Can't say that I do."

Jonas sighed.

"But he did drop this." Abner reached into his coat pocket and produced an expensive-looking handkerchief. The initials A.C. were embroidered onto it in swirly red stitching.

Jonas stared down at the soft white handkerchief. "Do you mind if I hang on to this?"

"Well," Abner grinned, "I was plannin' to use it to class up my ensemble. But I suppose I could be persuaded to part with it." He picked up his empty coffee mug and shook it lightly. Jonas smiled and poured him another cup.

Abner held the mug close to his face, closed his eyes, and inhaled deeply. "Mmm. That'll do just fine." He opened his eyes and smiled at Jonas again. "You go ahead and keep it. That scrap of cloth wouldn't have matched my jacket, anyhow."

Jonas stared at the handkerchief. A.C. He didn't know anyone with those initials. He traced the letters with his eyes. Over and over again. His jaw clenched as he did. Each stitch of its fabric scratched at his mind as he tried to picture the man it belonged to. He could feel his chest tighten at the thought. His brow furrowed as he glared at it.

"What are you planning to do when you find the man it belongs to?"

"Do?" Jonas looked up and shook his head. "Nothing. I just want to keep an eye out for who it might be."

Abner raised his eyebrow again.

"Really," Jonas insisted, relaxing his demeanor. "I just want to know who it was."

"So you can gently suggest he do his late night plant shopping elsewhere?"

Jonas laughed. "It's not like that. Sally is my friend and my neighbor. I'm just looking out for her. We don't know that the man you saw was a *suitor*. He could have been a lurker, or a thief, or some other ne'er-do-well."

Abner gave a small snort into his mug. "A ne'er-do-well with a handkerchief worth half a month's rent?"

Jonas shrugged. "Maybe."

Abner gave him a sympathetic smile. "You worry too much. End of the day, this other fella doesn't even show his face 'cept in the dead of night. That's not something a lady like Sally is going to put up with for long. Not when she's got you right across the street."

Jonas looked at the initials on the cloth. *A.C.* "I guess there's one thing I can be thankful for... at least I'm sure it wasn't Miller."

Abner laughed. "That man's not much for sneaking around. All his charm is out in the open. Everyone can see it. Beloved by all, that Dr. Miller is."

Jonas rolled his eyes.

"Oh, but don't let that bother you. You have your own brand of charm. It's more subtle. Some might even say, better. Not every woman wants a man oozing with charisma."

"Thanks, Abner," he said sarcastically.

"I'm pullin' your leg," Abner laughed. "Since when are you so jealous of the doctor? Sure everybody loves him, but everybody loves you too. You came up together. The whole town's two favorite sons. And if I'm being honest, I don't think his eyes on Sally are all that serious. The man flirts with everyone, but he's married to his work."

Jonas nodded and tucked the handkerchief into his pants pocket. Abner was right. Miller's favorite things in the world were money and success. He wasn't going to put in the time to court Sally. Not seriously. Not the way Jonas would.

Having that handkerchief out of his sight was like lifting a weight off of his chest. He suddenly felt silly for worrying about it at all. Jonas laughed, embarrassed. "You're right. I don't know what's gotten into me lately. I've been too focused on what other people have instead of what I have. And what I have," he gestured to the room around him, "is a pub that needs opening."

Jonas walked over to the window. The morning sun hit his skin; it was warm and calming, melting away his anxieties. No sooner had he propped the *open* sign up against the glass and the door swung open with his first customers of the morning. Early patrons were scarce, but a few folks in town liked to stop in for coffee on their way to Maeve's for breakfast, so he always had a pot ready for them.

Jonas smiled to himself as he began pouring coffee. He'd owned the pub for years, but every time that door opened, it brought a flutter of happiness and excitement to him. He really did love this place.

CHAPTER FOUR
The Pub

As the day wore on, all Jonas' regulars came and went, ordering drinks and exchanging pleasant conversation. Jonas loved days like this. The chilly winter air had let up a small bit. The sun was shining brightly through the window, bouncing off the beautiful wood sheen of the tables and chairs around the pub.

Jonas poured another round of drinks for the folks at the table in the corner and headed over with the tray.

"Jonas!" one of the women at the table shouted happily. She had short gray hair in tight curls and she was smiling broadly as he sat her drink in front of her.

"Here you are, Agnes," Jonas smiled. He passed the drinks out to the other women at the table with her. A group of five older women all laughing and cackling away. "You ladies staying out of trouble?"

"Not if we can help it!" one laughed, and they all joined in like a loud, jovial choir.

Jonas let out a small chuckle.

"There's that handsome smile!" Agnes said loudly.

Jonas rolled his eyes.

"Oh, you don't give yourself enough credit," Agnes argued. "Handsome, good natured, and a successful business owner. You're a catch, Jonas Decker."

Jonas raised an eyebrow and looked at her drink. "Maybe you've had too many of those."

"You make all the jokes you like, young man, but I hear things. The murmurs in the neighborhood," she said with a mysterious smile.

"Murmurs? Murmurs about what?"

"About you. And a certain plant shop owner."

"Sally?" Jonas asked.

Agnes nodded. "You should have heard how jealous the girls down at the market were when they found out you were spending time with her. Why, you've never heard ladies so bitter. The things they called her; it was scandalous."

"Over *me*?"

Agnes nodded.

"The market's on the wealthier side of town. I always figured the girls that work there would prefer someone more like Miller."

Agnes raised an eyebrow over her glass. "Nothing stopping them from liking the both of you."

Jonas shrugged and smiled. He found himself blushing a little at the idea of someone being jealous of him spending time with another woman.

"Oh, those girls down at the market," another woman scoffed. "Fickle little things, every one of them. Those aren't the type for our Jonas. Now Clara," she added coyly, "Clara is perfect for him. Classy, sophisticated, career type of lady."

"Oh," Agnes looked intrigued. "Clara? That would be quite a match," she smiled.

"Clara?" Jonas raised his brow. "Miller's nurse?"

"And your friend since you were children. I remember the three of you always running around town together." Agnes' grin widened.

"Oh, and after the life that girl's had," the other woman chimed in. "She could do with a bit of luck in her love life. Poor thing. Husband lost to illness. Widowed so young. No children. No job. Thank heavens for Dr. Miller. Steppin' in like he did, paying for her education, taking her on in his office. Still don't know why he didn't just marry her."

"Oh, Miriam!" Agnes waved a dismissive hand toward the other woman. "Clara and Dr. Miller aren't right for one another at all. Much too close their whole lives. Thick as thieves, those two. More like siblings than anything else. That's why he paid for all her nursing courses. He does things like that for the ones he's close to. Ask Jonas, he'll tell you."

Jonas shrugged. He'd honestly forgotten that Miller had done that for her. Jonas would have loved to think Miller had an ulterior motive, but there didn't seem to be one. Other than the entire town thinking he was some sort of saint. Which, for Miller, may have been reason enough.

Agnes smiled at Jonas again. "But you. You'd make a fine husband for a girl like Clara.

"What about Sally?" Jonas asked. "I thought the whole town was murmuring about her and I?"

"Oh, Sally seems a lovely sort. But she's much too new to the neighborhood. We don't know a thing about her," Agnes said. "Hardly had any time to snoop into her life at all," she added with a laugh.

"And those plants she keeps are dreadful," Miriam shuddered. "I'm frightened to even look around. I stopped by yesterday and I swear one of them tried to bite me!"

"You're mad," Agnes laughed. "Plants don't bite."

"Actually," Jonas began, "Sally's plants are a little... *aggressive*."

Agnes looked intrigued. "Really? Biting plants? Maybe I should get one of those. Keep the neighbor children from trampling through my vegetable patch. Or put it by the front door to keep the salesmen away!"

Jonas shook his head and laughed. As he walked away from the table, he could hear them all coming up with interesting places where they could put a guard plant. Jonas felt like it might soon become increasingly more dangerous to take a shortcut through one of their gardens. But at least Sally would be getting a flood of new customers.

As he walked back behind the counter, he thought about what the women had said. About him and Clara. He'd been so focused on Sally, the idea of anyone else seemed foreign and strange to him. Clara was beautiful and kind. She was a wonderful woman. And Agnes was right; they'd been friends since they were kids. But Clara had never shown any romantic interest in him as far as he could recall. Likely, the only place where Clara and Jonas would be a good match was in the inebriated imaginations of Agnes and her friends.

AS THE LAST CUSTOMERS headed out the door, Jonas turned the heavy lock and put the closed sign in the window. He cleared the last of the glasses from the tables and headed to his room in the back. It was late. Afternoons and nights were always fairly busy, but today he felt like he'd had more customers than usual. He was exhausted.

He took off his watch, a gift from his father when he'd first opened the pub. *A businessman needs to know the time*, he'd said when he gave it to him. Jonas smiled as he sat the watch on the nightstand. He emptied his pockets. A bit of loose change. A book of matches. A handkerchief.

It was the one Abner had found.

Jonas held the handkerchief in his hands, running his fingers along the stitching. Over and over again, as if tracing the man's initials would somehow conjure an image of his face. Surely Sally would have mentioned a suitor? At the very least, she would have spurned his own advances. Unless Abner was right, and there was some reason she couldn't allude to a man in her life? *No.* There had to be another explanation.

His mind flashed back to the man Sally had seen through the window. Could that have been who Abner saw? If so, it hardly seemed like a secret suitor. If Sally's expression was to be believed, she didn't seem pleased to see him at all.

Jonas shook his head. He was getting as bad as Abner; making up rumors and scandals in his own mind just to entertain himself. Abner had never actually seen the man *with* Sally. Not to mention his propensity to exaggerate.

The man Abner saw may have simply been walking by. He may have been a customer, checking to see if the shop was still open. It may have even been the landlord, sneaking a peek at how Sally was keeping the place up. Jonas' own landlord had always remained distant, but some were known to be less trusting, especially of a new tenant.

He tossed the handkerchief onto his nightstand and laid down in his bed. He pushed away every thought in his mind. Every thought but Sally. Her face was the only thing that lingered in the darkness behind his eyelids. He pictured every detail. Her warm smile. The dark curls of her hair. Those eyes, vibrant green and always shining. Even the necklace she always wore.

It was a beautiful gold locket with an ornate flower engraved across the surface. It gleamed in perfect placement, dangled across her soft white skin. Though, honestly, he was far more enchanted by the delicate skin it touched than by a piece of jewelry.

CHAPTER FIVE
The Intruder

The gentle jingle of the bell above the door echoed amongst the plants as Jonas entered Sally's shop. It was always a great deal warmer inside despite the winter chill outdoors. Something about the plants she kept made the air heavy and humid. It hit Jonas' lungs and he gave a small cough, catching Sally's attention.

"Mr. Deck- Jonas!" she quickly corrected. "Come look!" She motioned for him to join her at a small table near the center of the room. "Look at him!" She smiled broadly as she pointed to a large, vicious looking plant. It was covered in thick, thorned vines that writhed and wiggled in the pot. Its deep red flowers were covered in long, pointy spines.

Jonas watched as a fly landed on the petals. The flower snapped closed and wrapped itself tightly around the insect. He could see the silhouette of the fly through the thin red petals. It buzzed and squirmed, desperately trying to escape. But the flower petals constricted tighter and tighter around it, squeezing it down into the liquid at the bottom of the flower. Absorbing it.

Sally beamed. "Look at how well it's doing."

Jonas now realized that this was the tiny, sickly little plant from the day before. It had tripled in size overnight. He nodded, trying to feign enthusiasm. "Wow, that's really something. I can't believe how big it's gotten."

"It's eating so well now. That's the third fly it's caught this morning. Normally they wouldn't be so gluttonous, but since it's been ill, it needs all the nutrition it can get."

Sally stood admiring the plant as the bell rang out across the room.

The door swung open and a large, portly man trudged his way into the shop. His dark hair was combed over in an awkward attempt to hide his balding head. A huge belly protruded out from his body, covered by a blood-stained apron. His facial hair was patchy and uneven. It made its way down his neck, merging with the large clumps of hair on his chest and shoulders, jutting out from beneath his shirt collar and sleeves.

At nearly seven feet tall, he had to duck to keep from knocking his head against the doorjamb as he entered. Despite his enormous height, he was still easily twice the weight he should have been for a man of his stature.

"Gus!" Sally smiled.

"Morning, Sally."

She grabbed a large, mean-looking plant from behind the counter and brought it out to him. "I've got your new plant right here. Oh, I just know it's going to love living with you."

Gus owned the butcher shop next door to Jonas' pub. He was a good neighbor, though he did occasionally toss the odd bit of old meat into the alley, attracting more flies and pests than Jonas cared for. But it was rare and Gus always apologized. He was a good man and Jonas liked him.

Jonas was pleased to see so many neighbors supporting Sally and being so welcoming of her. Especially given the nature of her shop. A plant store was always welcome, but her flora were so unusual; Jonas had worried that people wouldn't like them. He realized now those concerns were unwarranted, as he watched Gus walk outside happily toting the barbed, snapping plant back to his butcher shop. Still, he had never thought of Gus as the plant loving type before.

Jonas looked across the street at the butcher shop. The front lawn was barren of any vegetation. Rocks and dirt filled the empty space on either side of the walkway.

"Sally, are you sure Gus knows how to take care of a plant?"

"I certainly hope so. He's bought several this week."

"Really?"

"Oh yes. He was one of my first customers." She laughed a little. "I'd barely unlocked the door my first morning here and there he was. Beaming with a friendly smile. Said his shop was in need of some cheerful plants to brighten things up."

Jonas looked out the window again and noticed a small gathering of customers outside his pub, waiting to be let in.

He looked at Sally. "Well, work calls. I'd best be going."

"Oh, I was hoping we could spend more time together today." She looked out the window towards his pub and gave him an understanding smile. "But I suppose I'm not the only one who wants your attention."

"Maybe tomorrow will be a slower day at the pub," Jonas said with a smile. And with another glance back at Sally, he walked out the door and crossed the street.

JONAS WIPED DOWN THE bar and cleared the last of the mugs and glasses from the empty tables. The street outside was dark and quiet as he tucked the *closed* sign into the corner of the window. His gaze lingered on Sally's shop. The lights were still on in the windows and the door seemed to be ajar. It seemed odd for her to still be open so late.

He turned out his own light and walked toward the back of the bar to the little room where he slept, but stopped just before he reached it. A scream echoed out from across the street, cutting through the quiet stillness of the night. And again. Another blood curdling echo rang out into the air. A woman's voice crying out for help. He turned and looked back toward the window.

Sally.

Jonas raced outside, feet hitting hard against the cobblestones beneath him as he ran. His heart pounded as he burst through the door and into Sally's shop. Broken flower pots littered the floor; a mess of potting soil and uprooted plants. But no sign of Sally.

Jonas heard footsteps behind him as Miller ran into the shop after him. "What's going on?" Miller demanded. "Where's Sally?"

Another sharp scream cut through the air. A crash of breaking glass and tumbling boxes. It was coming from a small room in the back. Jonas and Miller both raced behind the counter toward the sound.

An elderly man had a hold of her arm. He was clawing and grasping at her throat. His gnarled fingers wrapped around the chain of her locket. He pulled and tugged, yanking the chain harder and harder from her neck, but it stayed tightly fastened. He didn't seem to notice the chain cutting into his own fingers. His long, filthy nails scratched at her skin. His own blood trickled down his hand.

Jonas and Miller each grabbed him and tried to pry his grip from her. It was harder than Jonas expected. The man looked frail and weak, but he was strong. His grip was tight and his face was contorted in rage. He spat and frothed as he screamed in Sally's face, fingers still wrapped in her locket, pulling it tight against her throat.

"Harlot! Vile woman!" the man screamed in a coarse, raspy voice. "I'll end you!"

As they finally pulled him from Sally, he turned his attention to them. "Can you smell it on her?" His eyes were wild. "The rotting flesh."

Miller raised a quizzical eyebrow at Jonas. "One of your drunken patrons, I presume?"

"I've never seen him before." Jonas insisted. "Besides, I don't think he's drunk. I think he's gone mad."

The man writhed and wriggled, lunging toward Sally again. But he couldn't escape their grasp.

"It must stay closed! It must stay closed!" he raved at them as they dragged him through the store. He grabbed Jonas and Miller by their shirts and pulled them close to his face. "*It must stay closed,*" he said again through gritted teeth.

They pulled him to the front of the shop and tossed him into the street. Sally stood with them at the door, staring out at the man as he clambered to his feet. Her delicate neck was covered in deep red marks where the man had gouged her locket chain into her skin.

The man stood in the darkened street, staring at the three of them in the doorway. "You won't go unpunished. I've seen to it." He suddenly seemed quite sane and composed. Calm. Steely. Almost eerily so. "Your due will come. Everyone sees the rose..." He smiled. "No one thinks of the thorns." Without another word, he stepped away from them and disappeared into the shadows shrouding the opposite side of the street.

Jonas closed the door and helped Sally to a small chair on the other side of the room. "Are you alright?" he asked.

Her face was pale and her hands shook as she nodded. "I think so."

"Who on earth was that old fool?" Miller demanded.

"A madman," Sally answered. A look of disdain on her face.

"Do you know him?" Jonas asked.

She shook her head. "I didn't recognize him. I don't know why he would attack me like that. He burst in the door as I was locking up. Screaming and raging, mouth full of nonsense. He was a man possessed."

Miller slipped between Jonas and Sally, kneeling next to her and taking her hand in his own. "Oh, you poor thing. You're shaking. Let me get you a nice tonic. Something to help you sleep peacefully and wipe that man from your thoughts."

Sally smiled at him. "That's so kind of you, but I'll be alright."

"Are you certain you'll be safe here alone?" Miller asked, his voice filled with saccharin.

"Oh, I don't think he'll be back. Besides," she looked up and smiled at Jonas, "Jonas is right across the street. I'm certain I'll be safe."

"Yes, well, he does have quite a lot of experience when it comes to riffraff. I'll give you that," Miller said with a sour sneer. He stood and walked toward the door, stepping over the toppled plants and broken pots. "Well, I have patients to see in the morning, and they need me at my best. So, if you're well enough, I'll take my leave now."

"Yes, thank you so much for your help, Dr. Miller," Sally smiled and bid him goodnight.

Jonas walked behind the counter to the storeroom in the back. He pushed aside an empty rat trap and grabbed the broom and a small dustpan. Spilled soil and broken clay pots littered the showroom floor. Jonas began sweeping up the mess and sorting through the bits that could be salvaged. Sally brought out a stack of colorful new pots and rescued the fallen plants from the floor. The two of them worked together in silence, stopping every so often to smile at one another.

CHAPTER SIX
Taking Root

Jonas opened his eyes and rolled from the covers. A groggy fog filled his mind. His eyelids were still heavy and his body ached. He'd hardly slept at all. No matter how he tried, Jonas couldn't shake the image of that nightmarish man. Snarling like a rabid animal, clawing at Sally's flesh. What twisted logic could have led him to do such a thing? How could anyone wish harm on such a sweet, gentle creature as Sally Lockley?

He stumbled from his bed and into the pub. The dim light of morning shone through the large front window. He walked to the sturdy oak door, untwisted the lock, and swung it open.

"Alright, Abner, come on in. Get yourself warmed up."

Silence.

Jonas peeked his head out into the brisk air and looked around. Abner wasn't there. He stepped out, pulling his shirt tighter to his body as the cold of winter hit him. He looked down the street at the row of businesses, expecting to see Abner sitting near one of them. *Nothing.* He walked a few steps toward the alley that separated the pub from Gus' butcher shop next door. Jonas peered into the little pathway, but saw nothing stirring. It seemed Abner may have finally taken his advice and slept in his own bed for once instead of on the street somewhere.

He looked across the street, at all the little shops and stores that lined the way. There were people bustling happily on their way, wandering in and out of the shops along the cobblestone sidewalks. Maeve, the baker, was headed down the street with a large basket of bread. She must have been making a delivery. She didn't do that very often, but there were a few customers she'd make the effort for. The produce vendor from the next block over was hanging signs. Sale on cabbage. He even saw Gus walking into Sally's shop, probably buying another plant. But no sign of Abner.

Jonas hurried back into the pub, closing the door behind him. He shivered off the cold as the warm air of the room hit his body. The large clock on the wall behind the counter let out a small chime. Half past ten in the morning.

Jonas sighed. He'd missed the morning customers.

Despite getting very little sleep, he'd still somehow managed to sleep in. The afternoon crowd would be arriving soon and he was still barely awake. He put on a fresh pot of coffee and let it brew as he dressed and readied himself to face the day. He buttoned his waistcoat and smoothed the fabric against his chest. It held a few small stains and could benefit from a trip to the dry cleaners, but this wasn't the morning to worry about that. He strapped his watch to his wrist and headed over to the sink.

Jonas looked at his reflection in the mirror and groaned at the tired, scruffy image that met his eyes. He grabbed a palmful of wax and forced his ginger tangles into place. Most days, his hair seemed to have a mind of its own. Jonas thought keeping it short, like Miller's, would give him some control over it. But after every haircut, it felt like the moment he walked out of the barbershop, it was already tousled in all directions.

He stared into the mirror again. Better. The wax seemed to be holding, for now at least. He could certainly do with a shave, but there wasn't time for that. He grabbed a rag and polish from behind the bar and began shining the wood of the bar top and tables. A soft sheen glistened over the wood grain, beaming in the light from the window.

Jonas squinted as he peered through the glass. The sun was bright in the sky, casting a beautiful glow over Sally's plant shop. He felt a small tinge of jealousy each time a customer opened her door and walked inside. He desperately wanted to go and see her, but there wasn't time. Jonas looked down at his watch; ten minutes past eleven.

He looked around at the empty pub. Perhaps he did have a moment to pop over and see Sally before the afternoon crowd arrived. Jonas put on his coat, buttoning the middle clasp to hide the stains on his waistcoat, and headed across the street toward Sally's. He'd barely reached the sidewalk when the door swung open and the large shape of Gus appeared in the entryway. Gus stepped out of the shop, nearly plowing over the top of Jonas as he did.

"Morning, Gus."

"Oh. Morning, Decker." Gus had another one of Sally's plants cradled in his arm. It must have been the fourth or fifth one he'd bought from her.

Jonas smiled. "Another plant then?"

"Well... they're just so beautiful. And nice... and she smells good- I mean *they*. *They* smell good," he corrected. "The plants. Not Sally. Not that Sally doesn't smell good. She does. But I'm not smelling her if that's what you're thinking... I mean, obviously I-" Gus trailed off. "I should get back to my shop."

Jonas had never considered Gus a rival for Sally's affection. Though, now that he thought about it, he had been spending a lot of time in her shop and he'd certainly bought a lot of plants.

But still, Gus was just *Gus*. He wasn't attractive, or wealthy, or refined. He wasn't *Miller*. Miller was competition. Miller was a rival. All the same, it did bother him a little that Gus was making such obvious grabs at Sally's attention.

Jonas watched as Gus made the labored walk back to his shop, half out of breath by the time he made his way up the small staircase to his door. He certainly didn't seem threatening. But... what if Sally saw him differently? There was no telling what might catch a woman's attention. And she had seemed so happy to see Gus when he came in. Jonas stopped himself.

Surely he wasn't jealous of Gus? ...was he?

Jonas shook his head and tried to push the thought from his mind.

JONAS ENTERED THE PLANT shop expecting to find Sally in the same or worse condition as himself. A similar night of nightmares and sleeplessness. He saw her across the room, watering a row of plants.

"Good morning, Jonas!" she called out, happily.

She didn't seem tired or distressed at all. A rested, glowing Sally greeted him with a chipper smile. She looked lovely in a pale blue dress. Not a hair out of place. No sign of worry on her face. Even the gouges around her neck from her locket seemed to have completely vanished.

Jonas smiled. "You seem well today."

"Of course," Sally said. "It's a wonderful day. Full of life, wouldn't you say?"

Jonas nodded. "I suppose it is. Though I'd say last night was certainly unusual."

Sally nodded. "Yes. But thanks to you and Dr. Miller, we all came out of it unscathed."

"I see that, and I'm glad you're well. I thought that man had hurt you, the way he'd clawed at your skin and pulled at your necklace."

She put her hand protectively to her locket. "He was frightful. But thankfully, he didn't hurt me too badly. A bit of redness that was cleared by this morning."

"That's an interesting piece of jewelry," Jonas said with a gesture toward the locket she still clutched. "Something special, I take it?"

Sally nodded. "It means the world to me. It holds such special memories inside. I don't know what I would have done if he'd have damaged it."

Jonas gave her a smile. "I don't think you have to worry about that. It seems pretty strong to me. Honestly, I think that chain did more damage to him than he did to it."

She smiled back at him and released her grip from the locket. It hung loosely at her chest, glistening in the light from the window. Jonas had never paid the locket much attention until now. He'd noticed that she wore it, but not much else.

"It really seems to mean a lot to you. I suppose it holds an image of someone special?" He felt a small tinge of jealousy as soon as the words left his lips.

"Oh, yes, he's quite-" The door swung open behind them, with a small jingle from the bell above it. "Dr. Miller," Sally said with a smile. "How lovely to see you."

Miller smiled broadly at Sally. "Well, I found myself with some time between patients." He turned to Jonas. "Abner didn't arrive to his appointment this morning. Your fault, I suspect. His dependency on that swill you serve."

Jonas shook his head. "I haven't seen him today."

"Well, when he eventually stumbles through your door, would you kindly remind him that caring for his health is more important than catering to his vices?"

Jonas nodded. As much as he hated to side with Miller, he was right. Abner was frequently unwell and lived a life filled with bad habits. Even when no one in town would serve him, he always managed to have that flask in his pocket filled with something. He stayed out all night in all types of weather. Jonas couldn't count the number of times he'd opened his door in the morning and found Abner out there, asleep in the street.

Miller looked around the shop, then pulled a pocket watch from his vest and checked the time. "I should be heading out. Clara will have my hide if I'm late for another appointment."

"She keeps quite a reign on you," Sally said. "I feel like I hardly spend any time with you at all."

"A doctor is always in demand. And Clara makes sure I'm where I need to be. Which, right now, is on a house call with a patient that requires my attention." Miller turned to Jonas. "I was really just hoping I might catch Abner at your pub. When the door was locked, I suspected you were here." He looked out the window. "Speaking of which, it looks like you have people lined up outside, Decker. Might want to open up."

Jonas looked out the window. A couple of regulars were standing on the sidewalk near the pub. Miller headed out the door and held it open for Jonas.

"Coming, Decker?"

Jonas hesitated, looking back at Sally. "I'll... I'll open up in a bit."

Miller furrowed his brow and glanced across the street at the gathering patrons. "Are you sure it's a good idea to keep them waiting? They're paying customers."

"It'll be fine," Jonas insisted.

Miller shrugged and released his grip on the door. It swung closed and through the glass panes Jonas could see Miller heading down the sidewalk toward his office. Jonas turned back and looked at Sally.

"Anything you need before I head back to the pub?"

Sally smiled sweetly. "I wouldn't want to put you out. I know you have people waiting on you."

"It's alright. They can wait a bit. If there's something you need."

"Well," Sally's eyes flittered toward the room behind the counter. "It's just... there are some heavy pots in the back I can't seem to carry. I filled them with a bit too much soil and now I can't lift them to bring them out to the showroom."

Jonas smiled. "I think I can help with that."

He walked into the back room and spotted the large pots in the corner. Three beautifully decorated containers with huge plants already buried in their soil. Jonas hoisted the first one up and brought it out front, setting it near a window. It had rich green leaves that seemed to curl at his touch.

The second container held a tree-like plant with dark, almost black leaves.

"No sunlight for that one," Sally called out. "It likes the shade."

Jonas carried it over to a dark corner on the farthest side of the room, far from the window's light. "How's that?"

Sally smiled. "Perfect."

Jonas walked back into the little storeroom and headed toward the last plant. It was covered in bulbous purple pods. They were shiny. Almost wet looking. Jonas watched one of the pods open slightly as an insect buzzed nearby. He reached his hand out to touch it, but Sally quickly stopped him.

"I wouldn't," she said, gently grasping his wrist with her slender fingers.

As the pod opened, a sent filled the surrounding air. It was sweet. Almost too sweet. The insect seemed to notice it right away. It shifted direction and flew toward the plant, landing on the plump purple bud. The insect began to struggle and pull, but it couldn't fly away. Whatever the wet coating on the pod was, it was sticky, trapping the insect where it landed. It struggled, but it was too late.

"It secretes a corrosive pitch. Almost like sticky stomach acid. To you or me, it's a skin irritant. Painful. Itchy. Difficult to wash off." She leaned closer to the plant, admiring it. "But for the intended prey, it's death."

Jonas lifted the pot, careful not to touch any of the purple bulbs or let them brush against his clothes. He placed it on a large, sturdy looking table.

"That's wonderful, Jonas. Thank you so much. I don't know what I'd do without you."

Jonas smiled broadly at her. He felt his cheeks flush slightly at her words. "Well, I'd better be getting back over to the pub. Need to open up for the day."

Jonas headed out the door and crossed the street. The customers who'd been waiting were gone. It seemed they'd grown tired of waiting for Jonas to open the doors. Jonas sighed. The lost sales wouldn't be good for business. The pub was fairly popular in town, but it was expensive to run. Jonas needed every sale he could get.

But Sally needed his help. She needed *him*. Surely that was worth a few sales for the day.

CHAPTER SEVEN
The Storm

The street outside was darker than it should have been. Gray clouds filled the sky, blocking out any remaining sunlight. A thick, looming fog drifted and twisted its way through the streets. A shiver filled the air.

Jonas looked out the window. He could barely make out the silhouette of Sally's shop across the street. Everything was clouded, drenched in a billowing white fog that swirled in an airy ballet, and swallowed the world outside.

He'd never seen fog like this. It felt *alive*.

He saw the formless shapes of townsfolk walking down the street. Making their way home from work or shopping. Trying not to get caught in the coming storm. Jonas heard a faint crack of thunder in the distance. It hadn't made its way to them yet, but it was certainly trying. He looked around at the empty bar. No one was coming out in this weather.

"Might as well close up," he sighed.

He headed over to lock the door when a thought popped into his mind. *Abner.* Abner would be the only person in town foolish enough to be out in weather like this. What if he needed a place to stay? Jonas pulled his hand from the lock. *No harm in staying open a bit longer.*

THE EVENING WAS STILL early, but with the storm outside, Jonas knew he wouldn't be getting any customers. He could hear the wind whipping and the rain beating down on the roof as he sat at the bar, mindlessly sketching on a napkin.

Mostly images of Sally. Her wide, innocent eyes. Her full, pouty lips. Each curly tendril of her hair, as it fell down her neck and draped over her shoulders. He drew the chain and oval locket gracefully across her chest. The moment he'd finished sketching the locket, he caught himself glowering at it. That locket. The way she cradled it, loved it, worried about it being damaged. It was almost certainly a gift. Why else would she be so protective?

His heart sank a little at the thought. An expensive-looking locket and a man from her past who could afford such lavish gifts. Someone who still meant so much to her that she clung to his memory with such devotion.

Jonas wasn't sure how to compete with that.

The rain barreled hard against the window, echoing through the pub; amplifying the gloom he felt. He tossed the napkin sketches aside, annoyed with his own drawings. A locket shouldn't bother him. A past love shouldn't bother him. He hated that it did.

Jonas walked over to the window and watched the rain. The wet and fog darkened the world outside and masked the neighborhood from view. He had to squint to make anything out. But he could see *something;* something moving in the street.

There was someone outside. The rain was so heavy, Jonas couldn't make them out clearly, but there was definitely someone there. The empty shadow of a man pacing back and forth in front of the window.

Who would be out in this? Why wouldn't they just come in? He found himself suddenly uneasy. It took quite a bit to scare him, but the odd behavior was at least enough to make him lock the door.

Jonas walked over to the sturdy oak door and twisted the lock into place. It gave in with a loud click just as the knob began to jiggle. His heart raced. Whoever that man was, he was trying to get inside the pub. He didn't know why the idea of opening the door frightened him. The man's behavior, the unnatural fog; maybe it was the storm itself. But something in his mind wouldn't let him unlatch the door.

The jiggling stopped and Jonas felt his nerves ease. He turned and walked back toward the bar, but stopped when he heard a peculiar sound. A long, low squeak coming from the window behind him.

Jonas turned around slowly. His breath was shallow. His heart was racing. Adrenaline surged through his body.

A man stood at the window, drenched in rain and shrouded in dark clothing. Jonas could see nothing of what he looked like, except a single finger extended, writing something in the condensation on the window. Jonas' heart lurched in his chest and he gasped at the sight of him. Before he could do anything, the man stepped back into the fog and vanished from Jonas's view. Leaving behind only his message on the window glass. *Beware.*

THE MAN HAD LONG SINCE disappeared into the darkness, but Jonas still refused to pull his eyes away from the window. He sat on a stool at the bar and stared. He didn't know why it was bothering him so badly. Perhaps a lack of rest was making him more jumpy than usual. He had been having difficulty sleeping lately.

He was being silly. The man's behavior was odd, pacing in the fog, writing ominous messages on the window. But it wasn't dangerous. Jonas took a breath and stepped down from the barstool.

The doorknob jiggled again.

Was it him? Was he back? What did he want?

Jonas steadied his nerves and walked slowly toward the door. He wasn't going to let this man get the better of him. Not in his own pub. In his own home.

BAM! BAM! BAM!

The loud, wet banging of a person's palm hit heavy on the door.

Jonas jumped, startled at the sudden knock.

"Jonas! Are you there?"

A woman's voice?

Jonas unlatched the door and was greeted by a drenched and smiling face.

"Clara?" Jonas stepped aside and let her in out of the rain.

He peeked out into the street, but there was no sign of the shrouded man.

"You didn't see anyone else out there, did you? A man, maybe?" he asked as he closed and bolted the door.

Clara shook her head. "No. Though with the fog, I don't know that I'd be able to see my own hand in front of my face. I barely found your pub. Besides, who would be foolish enough to be out in this storm?"

Jonas smiled and raised an eyebrow. "Speaking of which, what are *you* doing out in this weather?"

"Flooding," she sighed. "The east side of town is having a time of it and it looks like the water is headed this way. We're all sorted at Dr. Miller's and he took care of Maeve at the bakery. I was on my way home and I thought I'd warn you. If you have any sandbags, you should probably use them."

Jonas nodded. "I appreciate it. Can I get you a drink or a cup of coffee?"

"I'd love to, but I can't. Dr. Miller is walking me home and we have some prescriptions to drop off on our way. A couple of patients weren't able to go out in the weather, and Dr. Miller volunteered to deliver them."

There was a light knock on the pub door. Jonas opened it to see Miller standing under an umbrella, looking bored. "If you're done here in the gin slums, Clara, we have patients waiting on us."

"Jefferson! *Really*?" Clara huffed. She only ever used his first name when she was annoyed with him.

Miller smiled. "I'm kidding." He flashed a smirk and wink toward Jonas. "Decker knows I'm only teasing, don't you, Decker?"

Jonas rolled his eyes. "Hilarious."

Miller put his umbrella over Clara as she walked outside with him. "Clara, dear, remind me to come by here tomorrow and bring Decker something to cure the mood he's been in lately."

Clara sighed and turned to Jonas. "It was lovely to see you, Jonas," she said with a sweet smile. He could hear them bickering as they disappeared into the rain.

"It's not my fault he's sour all the time," Miller defended.

"You could be nicer. He's our friend."

"I'm always nice. Ask anyone."

Jonas shook his head as he closed the door. The fact that Miller thought he was ever nice to Jonas was baffling. Though not as baffling as Clara thinking he and Miller were friends. She was a sweet woman, and she wanted everyone to get along. He couldn't fault her for that.

CHAPTER EIGHT
Missing and Found

Jonas made his way down the wet cobblestones toward the bakery down the street. The weather had cleared, but the eaves were still dripping and the air still had the sweet smell of rain. He passed all the familiar shops on his street; the chandler, the cobbler. Jonas stopped. A shop he didn't recognize. A ghastly little curiosity with an unfortunate-looking doll sitting in the window.

The Dreary Portent? What a gloomy name for a store.

Jonas shook his head and walked a few more paces to the bakery. The little bell chimed as he entered. The smell of fresh bread filled the air. It was warm and soothing. After the night he'd had, he welcomed anything comforting. He took another deep breath and smiled.

"Morning, Maeve," he called out to the red-haired woman behind the counter.

"Jonas!" she exclaimed with a broad grin. "Haven't seen you in days! Having your usual this morning?"

He gave a nod, and she handed him a large bundle wrapped in paper. A thick soft pastry, glazed on the outside and fluffy on the inside. He bit into it. The sugary topping melted into the breading, blending into a sweet delight.

"Did you see that new shop next door?" he asked.

Maeve nodded. "Strange little place, just popped up during the night."

"During the storm?"

She shrugged. "I suppose it must have. Was all empty and boarded up yesterday morning, then today it's filled with little oddities and a sign above the door."

"Have you met the owners yet?"

She shook her head. "No. Not seen a soul over there."

Their conversation was interrupted by a swarm of customers pouring in for their breakfast pastries. Maeve's regular morning crowd. She already had several of their orders wrapped and ready for them. He gave her a smile and a wave as he walked out the door.

Jonas left the bakery and headed back toward the pub. As he passed the little curiosity shop again, he peered in the window. It was filled with items, but the storefront was dark. They didn't seem to be open for business yet.

It might have been a bit odd, but it was nice to see a new shop in town. He'd be sure to welcome them to the block whenever they officially opened.

THE PUB WAS QUIET AS he returned through the door. Jonas didn't get many patrons until later in the afternoon, except for the few who'd already been by for their morning coffee, so he generally had the mornings to himself. He sat at the table next to the window and finished his pastry. He stared out onto the bright street at Sally's shop, or at least, he tried to. Large smudges on the window were distorting and obstructing his view of it.

The stranger's message from the night before. *Beware.* The words were gone, but they left a filmy smear where they had been.

He replayed it in his mind. The image of that man in the rain. The eerie fog swirling around him. The haunting message on his window. What could he have wanted? Was it someone's idea of a joke?

Jonas nearly jumped from his seat when the large oak door swung open unexpectedly. Even more surprising was the person who entered the pub. Miller stood, looking out of sorts and out of place.

Jonas got up from his seat at the table and walked behind the bar. He quickly started wiping down glasses, pretending to be busy.

"What can I do for you, Miller?"

Miller walked up to the bar and looked around the room. "Place is holding up. It's been a while since I've been in here."

"I don't recall you ever coming in here. Not the high and mighty Dr. Miller. No, he's too good for a place like this."

Miller sighed. "I'm not here to argue with you, Decker."

"Why are you here, then?"

"I'm here in a professional capacity."

Jonas shrugged and looked around the empty pub. "I don't see anyone in need of a doctor."

Miller shifted uncomfortably. "I'm not just a physician... I'm also the coroner."

Jonas furrowed his brow.

"It's Abner," Miller explained. "He turned up this morning. The storm flooded the alley across the street. It washed him out from wherever he'd tucked away to sleep."

"He's dead?"

Miller looked down somberly. "I'm afraid so."

"Do you know what happened to him?" Jonas asked.

Miller shook his head. "There wasn't much left of him to examine. But from what I could find, there was no sign of trauma or injury. He must have just got himself caught in the weather. Except..." Miller hesitated.

"Except what?"

"When was the last time you saw Abner?"

"A few days ago. Why?"

Miller nodded. "That's what I thought. That was the last time I saw him as well. I just... He couldn't have been dead for any longer than that... but his body... I've never seen anyone decay that quickly. He looked like he'd been dead for years."

"What do you mean?"

"He was just bones and withered skin piled inside his clothes. He was fragile to the touch. Several of his bones disintegrated into dust when I tried to examine him."

"Are you sure it was him?"

Miller nodded again. "I didn't realize it until I examined the skull. I'd done some dental work for Abner last summer. Three gold teeth in the back of his mouth. There they were, in the same place as Abner's. Then I checked the bundle of tattered clothes he was wrapped in. That's when I found that flask he always carried; monogrammed with his initials."

Jonas shook his head in disbelief. "Thank you for letting me know."

"Abner didn't have any next of kin. I thought you were probably the person he was closest to."

Jonas smiled sadly. A somber crackle in his voice. "You're probably right. Even when I wouldn't serve him, he still spent all his time in here. I knew something was wrong when I hadn't seen him, but I never thought this..."

"I'm sorry," Miller said. "He was a good old man."

Jonas pulled out two shot glasses and grabbed a bottle from the top shelf. He filled both glasses and slid one to Miller. "To Abner."

Miller took the other glass. "To Abner."

Jonas was a little surprised that Miller took the drink. He'd never once been to the pub in all the years it had been open. Most of his snide remarks mocked Jonas' role in town as a barkeep. But this clearly wasn't a normal day for him. Jonas didn't really understand the science of it all, but he knew Miller did. And the state they found Abner in really seemed to unnerve him; enough that he was willing to stand at the bar and drink with Jonas.

It was an odd moment for the two of them. A temporary truce to their rivalry. It was nice, familiar even. Like maybe there had been a time in their past when they were almost friends. It was just a feeling. A whisper of a memory, perhaps from childhood. They did grow up together, after all; it was conceivable that they'd had some pleasant exchanges. Even if Jonas couldn't recall that they ever had.

Though Jonas was certain they'd be back to their normal nature in no time. Snide remarks and glowering looks. But for now, the peace was welcome, no matter how fleeting.

NEWS OF ABNER'S DEATH spread through the neighborhood. Though the odd condition of his body was kept quiet. Abner didn't have any family, but most of the neighborhood turned up for the funeral. They gathered around the gravesite, staring down at the cold earth and the casket deep below them.

They buried Abner in the nicest part of the cemetery. Rather, they buried a casket filled with bone dust and a monogrammed flask. The funeral was fancier than Abner would have chosen, but with Miller footing the bill, Jonas could hardly object. Miller paid for everything; the burial, the food, he even opened a tab at Jonas' pub so everyone could drink on his dime. A small part of Jonas wanted to be annoyed. Wanted to accuse him of showing off his wealth. But the better part of himself prevailed.

It was a gloomy scene around the grave. Mourners bid their last farewell to a beloved friend. Agnes and Miriam were huddled with their friends. Maeve gave a sad sigh and Gus muttered a few words goodbye.

Miller stood with his arm around Clara as she sobbed on his shoulder.

"Was it being out in the weather that took him?" Clara asked.

Miller looked uncomfortable. "Come now, Clara, let's not talk about that right now."

"But you examined him, surely you-"

"Clara, dear," Miller interrupted gently. He seemed desperate not to talk about Abner's cause of death. "We really should all be heading over to Decker's pub now." He looked toward Jonas. "Shouldn't we?"

Jonas nodded. "Yes, drinks and food. Maeve set out pastries. Everyone's welcome."

An excited murmur spread through the crowd as they all headed toward the pub. The promise of Maeve's food seemed to grab everyone's attention. Even Clara perked up a bit and headed over with the rest of the group.

Miller looked relieved. He really must have been desperate if he was encouraging people to go to the pub. Miller hung back, staring at the gravesite. He still seemed troubled.

"You alright?" Jonas asked.

"I didn't tell anyone about how Abner was found," Miller said, without looking up. "Most people in town wouldn't be bothered, but Clara would recognize the strangeness of it all. She'd have more questions and I have no answers. The condition he was in..." Miller shook his head. "I don't know."

"You're going to have to tell her something. Maeve's pastries will only distract her for so long."

Miller smiled. "I don't know. I think a daily trip to the bakery might buy me a few weeks."

"Maybe," Jonas laughed. "Speaking of which, we should probably head over there. People will be expecting me to serve drinks and since you're paying for everything, you should probably be a part of it."

Jonas and Miller headed together toward his pub. It was a quiet walk, but Jonas had to admit it wasn't entirely unpleasant. Maybe it was because they were grieving, but Miller seemed more personable and Jonas' animosity toward him felt lighter. No matter the reason, Jonas was happy for the shift in mood between them.

CHAPTER NINE
Under The Weather

It had been a few days since Abner's funeral, and life was beginning to return to normal. But it was still a somber morning for Jonas. The day shone gray and overcast through the clouds. It was more than just the weather and losing Abner. There was an ache to his bones. He was tired. And there was a feeling inside him, something deep and primal plucking at his nerves. Dread. He couldn't put his finger on it. Just a feeling that was there, but he didn't know why.

He stood at the bar, wiping it down with an old rag. The motion and repetition were soothing. The damp cloth swirled back and forth across the polished wood. Tiny streaks of water trailed behind it, then dried up and vanished a moment later. It was peaceful... until it wasn't.

The oak door swung open, and Miller stepped into the pub. Annoyed and huffy. He hadn't said a word yet, but his puffed chest and tight jaw spoke volumes about his mood. Jonas could already tell his day wasn't going to be getting any better.

"What's bothering you?" Jonas asked, looking up from the bar.

"Do you mind explaining why I found this slipped under my office door this morning?" He tossed a hand written note onto the bar. "I thought we were past this, Decker? Threats? *Really?*"

Jonas furrowed his brow as he picked up the note and read it. Thick, black letters were scrawled across the paper. A cryptic warning penned in ink.

Beware Sally Lockley.

"I don't know what's gotten into you lately, Decker, but I suggest you straighten yourself out."

"This wasn't me!" Jonas argued, but Miller looked thoroughly unconvinced.

"You may think this sort of behavior gains you something, but mark my words, your petty jealousy is going to be your undoing with her one day."

Miller stormed out of the pub, slamming the oak door behind him. It seemed their tentative truce was over.

"How *dare* he?" Jonas huffed to the empty room. "How *dare* he come into *my* pub and accuse me of sending him some anonymous note? The *nerve* of that man."

He grabbed the note from the bar and ripped it angrily in half, tossing the pieces on the floor. He sat at the table near the window and stared out onto the street. Jonas watched the people bustling from shop to shop and exhaled in a long quivering breath, some of his ire subsiding. He glanced down at the torn paper. Only one half had landed face up.

Beware.

Jonas bent down and picked it up. He held it tightly in his hand and looked out the window at Sally's shop. He remembered the man outside during the storm, and the message written on the glass. *Beware.*

It wasn't just some madman in the night. It was someone *threatening* him. He hadn't put it together at first, but it was the only thing that made sense. He knew he hadn't written the note, and he was certain Miller wasn't the one who wrote the message on his window.

Someone out there wanted him and Miller to both stay away from Sally. His face hardened, and he crumpled the scrap of paper in his fist, tossing it aside. Whoever was doing this, they weren't going to keep Jonas away from her so easily.

Jonas looked around the pub. Small, dingy, everything looked worn and shabby. He looked out the window. No matter how many times he cleaned the glass, it never seemed to let in enough light. Jonas stared at Sally's shop across the way. It was bright and inviting. Clean. Pristine. Full of life and light.

That's where he wanted to be.

That's where he *should* be.

Not in this miserable hole in the wall; in a bright, beautiful shop filled with plants and happiness... and Sally.

That settled it. No one was going to scare him away from her. Jonas locked the pub door and headed across the street. Where he belonged.

JONAS PUSHED THE DOOR open and smiled as he heard the familiar ring of the bell above the door. The thick, fragrant air of Sally's shop hit his senses the moment he walked in. Sally was fussing with a wilted plant near the window. There wasn't much light coming through the clouds, and she seemed to be having trouble finding a sunny place to put it.

Jonas looked around the shop and noticed that many of the plants seemed to be weak and wilting. But it wasn't just them. Sally, too, looked a bit listless and pale. She smiled as she caught sight of him. Dark circles had overtaken her eyes.

"Are you alright?" Jonas asked.

"Oh, I'm just a bit under the weather. I've been so worried about my poor plants, I just haven't been able to recover my own health." She gestured around the room toward the sickly plants.

"Yes, I see. They don't look well at all. Is there anything I can do?"

Sally shook her head. "They need food. The special plant food I feed them. I had a new batch, but the storeroom flooded during the storm. If only I had put it in the metal canister like I usually do, but I left it on the floor and the next morning the whole bag had been washed away through the grate and out into the alley. The entire thing, gone."

"Can you get more?"

"I suppose I'll have to. It's just such a shame. I do hate to waste good plant food." She sighed heavily. She looked so tired.

"There's nothing you can do for the plants today. Why don't you close up early and get some rest?"

Sally looked around the room. "You're probably right. I don't imagine I'll sell many plants with them looking like this, anyway. Hopefully, I'll have some food for them tomorrow."

Jonas smiled at her. "And until then, there's no point in you being down here worrying about them. You should be asleep in your bed. I'll help you close up."

Sally smiled, weakly. "You do take such good care of me."

Jonas hardly had time to enjoy her sweet words when the bell above the door let out a gentle chime, interrupting their moment together.

Gus entered the shop with heavy footsteps and a furrowed brow. He held one of his new plants in his hand. Its leaves were withered, its blooms were wilted.

"Oh dear. Gus, what happened?"

Gus shook his head. "Don't know. Been watering it. Getting lots of sunlight. Don't know where I went wrong."

"Have you been feeding it?" Sally asked, still examining the little plant.

Gus looked confused.

"All those leftover bits of meat you have lying around? Have you been feeding them to the plants?"

"Meat?" Gus still looked puzzled. "To a plant?"

"They're carnivorous plants," Sally explained. "They eat meat. That's why I thought they'd be so happy with you in your shop."

"Oh!" Gus suddenly seemed to understand. He marveled at the little plant. "Well, I'll be. A meat eater, huh?"

Sally nodded. "Just cut up small pieces of leftover meat and place them right here." She pointed to the large spiked petals of the flowers. "It should perk up in no time."

Jonas' suspicions of Gus had been correct. He didn't have the faintest idea how to care for a plant. All his trips to the shop, all the plants he'd been buying to *brighten up his butcher shop*. It had all been attempts to impress Sally. He was trying to trick her into thinking they had something in common. That he was interested in her plants and her shop.

Jonas was seeing Gus in a whole new light. Beneath that bumbling oafish facade lurked a cunning man. A man with designs on sweet Sally's heart. Jonas couldn't blame him, but he wasn't going to just stand back and allow it.

"Well, I'm certainly glad that's sorted," Jonas said smiling and opening the door. "But I'm afraid Sally's a bit under the weather today, so I'm helping her close up early."

"Is there anything I can do for you?" Gus asked Sally.

"Oh, no. I don't think so, Gus." She smiled at him. "Jonas is taking good care of me."

"I'm right across the street," Gus said, heading out the door. "Anything you need. You come get me."

"I certainly will," Sally said warmly.

Jonas shut the door and put the closed sign in the window.

JONAS HELPED SALLY up the staircase to her room. She crawled, exhausted, into her bed. It seemed she didn't even have the strength the change into her nightclothes. The dark circles beneath her eyes had grown heavier, draining the color from her cheeks and the sparkle from her eyes.

"Jonas, darling?" Her voice was beginning to strain. "Could you do me a favor?"

"Of course. Anything."

"Could you go and fetch Dr. Miller from his office in the morning?"

"Miller?" Jonas' skin burned at the mention of his name. "Are you sure you need him?"

"I really do think it's time I saw the doctor. I've tried everything else, but I've exhausted all the other remedies I could find. He really is the only option."

Jonas' mind raced. Surely there was something else. Someone else. Anyone other than Miller that could help her. Miller was the only doctor in the neighborhood, but maybe there was a visiting doctor at the hospital. Or maybe Sally didn't need a doctor at all. Maybe a nurse instead. That was it! A nurse! Clara.

Jonas smiled and pulled the covers up around Sally, making sure she was comfortable. "How about I head out to his office now?

His nurse, Clara, will be there and I can bring her by to take a look at you."

"No!" Sally shouted, sitting up in her bed.

Jonas jumped back, surprised by her reaction.

She took a deep breath and recovered herself. "I'm sorry. I don't mean to be so emotional. It's just, it must be Dr. Miller. He's really the only one that can help me."

Jonas nodded and left her room, a little shaken by her outburst. It went against every instinct in his body. But if she insisted on seeing Miller, Jonas had no choice but to give her what she needed.

CHAPTER TEN
The House Call

The morning air was cold and stung Jonas' cheeks as he walked down the street toward Miller's office. It was early, and the shops were only just starting to open. There was no one out yet. The neighborhood was quiet, peaceful; almost eerily so. Which made it all the more noticeable when he heard voices.

Miller was standing outside his office having an intense conversation with a man Jonas had never seen before. He wore a top hat and a custom suit. A small rose was embroidered on his lapel.

"It must stay closed," the man said sternly.

Miller furrowed his brow as the man vanished down the alleyway and out of sight.

"What do you want, Decker?" Miller asked, turning to face him.

"It's Sally," Jonas said. "She's ill."

"Sally?" Miller hesitated. He looked conflicted. "I... I can't see her."

"You have to. Miller, she needs your help. You're angry with me. Don't take that out on her."

Miller shook his head. "I'm-"

"I didn't write that note!" Jonas argued.

"No. I know that, Decker. I just-" he glanced down the alley where the man had disappeared. "We need to talk."

"Fine. We can talk later. But Sally's ill now."

Miller looked agitated. "I really think you and I should talk first. Why don't you come inside?" He gestured toward his office.

Jonas heaved an irritated sigh. "I can't. I have to get back to her. The only reason I left her side was to get you."

Poor, frail Sally, wasting away in her bed; it was all he could think of. Why wasn't Miller more concerned? Why didn't he see how urgent this was? Jonas wasn't happy about Miller being near Sally, but he was a doctor and she was ill. She'd asked for him.

"If it makes you feel better, I'll send Clara to look after her while we talk. Then Sally won't be alone. She'll be in good hands."

"She needs *you*," Jonas said. "I'm not happy with the fact that her health relies on you, but it does. I tried to bring Clara round yesterday, but Sally wouldn't have it. She said she needed you. That you were the only one who could help her."

Miller furrowed his brow. "Me, *specifically?*"

Jonas nodded. He expected Miller to look flattered or smug. But he didn't. He just looked toward the alleyway again, his brow still furrowed.

"Fine. I'll come round this afternoon."

Jonas smiled, relieved. "Good. I'll let her know you're coming."

DR. MILLER WALKED IN the door with all his usual smugness and superiority. He was carrying a black leather doctor's bag and wearing a suit that probably cost more than Jonas made in a month.

"Someone call for a doctor?"

Jonas stepped aside and let him into the room. "She's been ill for a few days now. It came on slowly, but now she can barely leave her bed."

"Don't worry, Decker, I'll fix her right up," he said with a cold smile. "It's a nice day out. Why don't you take a walk and leave us to it?"

Miller was clearly still angry about the note. It was hardly fair. Jonas *hadn't* written it. On the street in front of his office, he'd claimed to believe Jonas. But now, in the light of Sally's hallway, it was written all over Miller's face; that look of accusation. Jonas' word should have been good enough. If Miller refused to believe him, that was his own issue.

"A little privacy for the patient, Decker?" Miller said, motioning again for Jonas to leave the room.

Jonas wanted to object, but he didn't have the chance.

"Oh yes, darling. That's a lovely idea," Sally agreed weakly. "I'd be so grateful if you would tend to my plants. I haven't been able to care for them properly in days. They must be so wilted and weak."

Jonas sighed. Every hair on the back of his neck was raised. Everything in his body screamed for him not to leave them alone together. But he knew how much she loved those plants. And she was trusting him with their care. He couldn't deny her that.

"Fine." Jonas nodded, stepping out into the hallway. "But I'll be right downstairs if you need me."

Dr. Miller sat his bag down on the bed near Sally. "Perhaps you should consider going back across the street and tending to your own pub," he said snidely. "People have been checking for it to open all day. Hardly a good way to run a business, Decker."

Jonas opened his mouth to retort, but Miller was already closing the bedroom door.

JONAS LOOKED OVER THE sea of carnivorous-looking plants around the shop. Several of them had succumbed to wilting leaves and a droopy demeanor. The insects around the shop didn't seem to be enough to sustain them. Sally still hadn't gotten the new batch of plant food, but at least he could make sure they had enough water.

Jonas looked around, searching for the watering can, but there didn't seem to be any sign of it. He was sure he'd seen it behind the counter the last time he'd been there. But all he found was a crate filled with potting tools, a stack of books on caring for exotic plants, and a large box he couldn't see inside of.

He opened the box, but there was no watering can inside. Instead, it was filled with scrapbooks and photographs, mementos of Sally's past and travels. Part of him wanted to look through them, but he thought better of it. She trusted him.

He pushed the box aside and heard a loud snap ring out from behind it. Jonas looked behind the box. A rat trap. It was empty. Hitting it with the box must have sprung the trap.

Jonas bent down to reset it but stopped and furrowed his brow. A second one sat just a few feet away. And a third. And a fourth. The whole wall of the room was lined with them, like Sally was expecting an army of rodents to sneak in through the window.

It seemed odd that she should be having such an infestation. He lived right across the street and hardly caught sight of any vermin at all. Unless, of course, Gus left a batch of old meat in the alley for the trash collection. On those days, he was likely to see all manner of creatures rummaging around. But he'd never caught one inside the pub.

Perhaps rats were just more attracted to plants than they were to ale. Or maybe the warmth of Sally's shop was more inviting during the cold winter nights. Her shop certainly was warm. More so than his pub, or even the bakery. Even now, he could feel it. A gentle heat emanating from the plants. It made the air thick.

Jonas didn't know much about plants, but he'd never heard of one being so warm. These plants clearly weren't used to this environment. Cold winters, scarce insects, and a lack of sunlight, weren't doing them any favors. Even the ones sitting in the window were wilted.

The window.

There it was, the watering can, sitting in the window next to the flowerpots. Sally must have been watering yesterday before they closed the shop. He walked over and grabbed the can, still filled with water.

Jonas glanced out the window and was surprised to see several people milling around outside his pub. He thought Miller had just been trying to get rid of him, but it seemed people really were checking to see if it was open. He really did need to open up if he was going to have any chance of paying his vendors this month. There were Agnes and Miriam, with all their friends. Lots of other folks Jonas recognized, too.

And one he didn't.

A man. He looked out of place in an expensive suit and hat. He stood away from the others, awkwardly checking his watch. Jonas leaned closer to the window. On a second look, he actually did recognize him. It was the man Miller had been talking to outside his office that morning. The man with the rose embroidered on his lapel. What could he want? Probably looking for Miller.

Miller.

Upstairs. Alone with Sally. It made his skin shiver and the hairs stand up on his arms. He hated the thought of it. He looked outside again at the small crowd forming around the pub door. They'd have to wait. He couldn't just leave Sally when she was ill. She needed him. She was depending on him.

JONAS FINISHED WATERING the plants and tidying up the shop and headed back upstairs to check on Sally. Her bedroom door was open. He peeked in and saw her laying in her bed, no sign of Miller.

Sally opened her eyes and smiled weakly. "Jonas."

He walked to her bedside and held her hand. "Where's Miller?" he asked.

"Gone," she said plainly. "He left rather quickly. Barely a word."

"Odd, I didn't hear him leave. You'd think I would have heard the door."

She smiled again. "Perhaps your mind was elsewhere."

Jonas nodded. He did find himself daydreaming more often than usual. Generally about Sally. Her face. Her smile. Her laugh. Sometimes just about being near her.

"Did he at least give you something to help you recover?"

She pointed to a small bottle of tonic sitting on her nightstand. "That, and a good night's rest, and I should be right as rain by morning."

Jonas smiled at her. "I should probably let you get to sleep then."

He stepped out of the room and started to close the door behind him, stopping for a moment to look back and admire the sleeping Sally. She was bundled in her covers. Eyes closed. Hand clenching tightly to the locket around her neck. *That locket*. It meant so much to her. Or rather, whoever was inside it meant so much to her.

His teeth clenched and his jaw tightened as he stared at the locket. It peeked out between her slender fingers, mocking him. He quickly closed the door and left.

CHAPTER ELEVEN
Mulch & Feed

Sally's health made a dramatic improvement by the next morning. Her color returned, her smile brightened, her eyes were back to their beautiful emerald green. Whatever Miller gave her, it worked.

"The new plant food just came in," Sally said with a chipper ring to her voice. "It's a special blend. Incredibly hard to get a hold of."

Jonas smiled. He'd never really had an interest in plants, but something about her enthusiasm was infectious. "Is that the food that makes them triple in size overnight?"

She nodded. "They really love it. I'm glad I could get my hands on some. Especially after that storm last week destroyed the bag I had. Such a waste."

"But you have a new bag now, and I think these little guys will be happy to see it." He gestured towards the wilting leaves of a nearby plant.

"Would you like to help me feed them today?" she asked.

"I'd love to." Jonas wasn't lying. He really did love helping her around the shop. Though it was more likely spending time with Sally than anything to do with the plants.

He followed her to the storage room, where a large metal canister sat alone on the shelf. As he lifted it up, he heard a loud snap from behind a stack of boxes. Another rat trap. She really did seem to have quite a rat problem. He started to look behind the boxes, but Sally stopped him.

"No, no. Don't worry about that. I'll handle it later," she said, grabbing him by the arm and leading him toward the door. "Let's feed the plants. It's better while the food is fresh."

Jonas opened the canister and looked inside. It was a cream-colored powder with some small, hard chunks scattered throughout. He picked one up, and it crumbled away in his fingers. He grabbed the small metal scoop from the canister and began sprinkling the mixture into the pots.

"Only the carnivorous ones," she instructed. "This food is special, just for them."

After each scoop, Sally moistened the soil with the watering can, assuring the nutrients would seep in to the roots. She lovingly wiped splashes of water from the leaves with a soft dishcloth and spoke to each plant as she did. Sweet little whispers of, *you're going to love this new food,* and *you'll feel much better once you've eaten.*

Jonas reached the scoop in again, but this time something odd was poking out of the top of the powder. It wasn't hard like the other chunks; it was softer and didn't deteriorate at his touch. He pulled the small gray piece of material from the mixture and showed it to Sally. It was soft and leather-like.

"What is this?"

Sally grabbed the shriveled bit of leather away from him and tossed it aside. "Just a piece of the bag it came in," she explained. "A bit must have fallen in when I cut it open."

"It comes in a leather bag?"

She nodded. "It does. I told you, it's very special."

Jonas fed the last of the plants and closed the metal canister. He looked around the shop; they were already starting to perk up. Soon they'd be back to full health, catching bugs on their own.

He watched as a fly landed on a particularly frightening looking plant. It was the only one in the shop that didn't seem to be wilted or withered at all. On the contrary, its blooms were full, its leaves were green, it seemed to be thriving. The fly wandered around on the leaves for a moment, then happily buzzed away.

"Is there something wrong with that plant?" Jonas asked.

Sally furrowed her brow and looked the plant over carefully. "It seems fine. Why do you ask?"

"A fly landed on there and it didn't do anything. Isn't that what it eats?"

"Yes, but this plant just ate this morning. She's the only one in the shop that's been managing to catch her own food. The insects just can't stay away from her." Sally smiled. "But she's smart. She knows how to bide her time, to make sure her meals count. If she's especially hungry or weak, she might opt for an easy meal; anything that happens to land nearby. But this variety is clever. She knows that the better option is to let the fly feed on her nectar. Each time the fly returns for a taste, it grows slower and sweeter, its senses dulling to the danger."

The fly buzzed around and returned to the leaf. Still, the plant didn't strike, allowing it to flitter away again.

Sally beamed at the little plant. "You see? The flower lets the insect fatten, until it's rich and juicy, gorged on the flower's honey. It makes for a much more delightful meal that way."

Jonas never knew how unsettling a plant could be. He'd never thought of them as predators. Until Sally moved in, he'd never even heard of a carnivorous plant before. Though they were unnerving, he had to admit they were interesting and, in their own way, beautiful.

JONAS WATCHED SALLY as she lovingly tended to the last of the plants. She leaned over, pouring water into the pots. Her soft curls fell around her face and her locket dangled from her chest, hovering near the petals of one of the nearby plants.

Jonas' fists clenched and his shoulders tightened. He could feel his mood sour the minute he saw it. *That locket.* It was mocking him. Hiding the secrets of her past behind a small etched flower of gold. Some secret love.

The thought of this man from her past still holding a place in her heart burned in his mind. A stranger intruding on the love that should belong to him. That nameless, faceless memory hiding within a locket.

But he wasn't faceless.

There was someone in there. He hated not knowing who she was keeping from him. They shouldn't have secrets. There shouldn't be a past love holding onto her so tightly, wedging its way between her and Jonas. It felt like the last barrier keeping them from truly being together. The last thing looming over them. Perhaps if he could just convince Sally to tell him more about the man, the feeling would vanish.

"That locket you wear," Jonas began awkwardly. "You mentioned it held the image of someone special. But you never said who."

Sally smiled coyly. "Didn't I?"

Jonas shook his head. "I know it's not my business and I understand if you don't feel comfortable sharing all of your past with me yet. But I'd like it if you would."

"It's nothing for you to worry about, darling. Just someone that sustained me through a difficult time. He helped me when I needed him. But that was the past. He is in the past. She smiled at Jonas. You are the future."

Jonas sighed, discouraged by her evasiveness.

"You aren't threatened by it are you?"

Jonas shook his head. "Of course not. I was just curious. That's all."

It would be ridiculous for him to be threatened by a necklace. A silly little bauble she wore around her neck. Every day.

Every. Single. Day.

That wouldn't be rational at all.

CHAPTER TWELVE
Hidden Pictures

"**J**onas, darling. Could you do me a favor and watch the shop for a moment? I need to dispose of something." She tried to keep it out of sight, but Jonas could see the edge of a rat trap behind her back.

"Would you prefer I take that out to the trash fo-"

"No, no. I've got it," Sally insisted.

"Alright. I'll just mind the counter for you, then."

Sally smiled and disappeared down a hallway at the back of the shop. Jonas had never been back there, but he assumed it must have led to the alley. Where else would she be going with a dead rat?

The store was quiet except for the gentle rustling of vines, like ropes rubbing against one another as they wound and twisted themselves across the shelves and counter-tops. He pushed a few aside and made his way to the register. He nearly tripped as he did, stumbling over a box covered in stray vines that had made their way behind the counter.

Jonas picked up the box, unwinding it from their grasp and sat it near the back wall. He recognized it. It was the box filled with Sally's scrapbooks... and pictures. He could see the corners of photographs and old tintypes sticking out the edge of the books. Old friends? Past loves? Maybe even the man from the locket.

His curiosity itched at his fingertips. He ran his hand across the topmost scrapbook. There was no point in snooping through her things. He didn't even know what the man looked like. He certainly wouldn't recognize him. Unless...

A horrible thought stirred in Jonas' mind. What if her past wasn't as far away as he'd thought?

What if he was someone in their lives?

Jonas couldn't stand the idea that this person might still be around her. Maybe that was why she refused to say anything about him. Maybe he was someone Jonas knew. Someone from town? But who? The thought seared through him. He had to know.

Though maybe he didn't need to see in the locket. Surely that wasn't the only picture she kept of him. If he could just steal a peek at the scrapbooks...

Once he saw that the only pictures she had were of unfamiliar faces, strangers she'd likely never see again, he'd be able to let it go. He'd never have to think of it again.

He'd be able to let her have her memories... once he had his peace of mind.

Jonas peeked down the hallway. No sign of Sally yet. He grabbed the scrapbook and quickly started going through it. The book was filled with notes and letters, adoring poems about her beauty, declarations of love penned on fancy stationery. There were postcards and souvenirs from all sorts of exotic places that Jonas had never heard of.

As expected, he also found a few photographs sprinkled throughout the pages. Pictures of Sally with past friends. She was always wearing that locket. In every picture, no matter who she stood next to, that ridiculous locket was always strung around her neck. Not a single one without it. If he could find a picture where she didn't have it, perhaps that would help him figure out which man had given it to her. But no luck. In every photograph, there it was, gleaming center stage across her perfect skin.

Aside from that locket plaguing every picture, most of the photographs seemed quite ordinary. Filled with people he'd never seen before and places he'd never been.

But one picture did stand out. Though Jonas couldn't put his finger on why. He picked up the scrapbook and examined the photograph closer.

Sally was standing near a dashing-looking young man. He was well dressed and handsome. Jonas felt a small tinge of jealousy. The man stared out from the photo. Expensive suit. Fancy watch. A monogrammed handkerchief sticking up from his pocket; the letters A.C. stitched onto it.

A.C.

Jonas looked down at the bottom of the picture at a handwritten note.

Mister Arthur Cutmore

Jonas remembered the handkerchief that someone had dropped outside Sally's shop. The one embroidered with the letters A.C. Could it have been him? He stared closer at the picture. Something was gnawing at him. There was something about this man. He was... *familiar.*

That strong jaw. Those stern looking eyes. He'd seen that face before. Jonas racked his brain. Trying to remember. Then it came to him.

The old man.

The one who attacked Sally in her shop that night. He had that same jaw, those same eyes. He must have been related to Mr. Cutmore. His father, perhaps? But why would an old suitor's father track Sally down and attack her? And why would she say she didn't know him?

Jonas heard the sound of the door coming from down the hallway. Sally was back. He pulled the picture from the scrapbook and slipped it into his pocket, then packed away the rest of her things and slid the box under the counter.

CHAPTER THIRTEEN
The Missing Man

Jonas walked hastily down the street. He stared at the cobblestones beneath his feet, lost in his own thoughts as he headed towards the old brick building on the east side of town. Perfectly trimmed shrubberies sat on either side of a large entryway. A wooden sign was fastened to the bricks, stern-looking letters engraved across its surface. *Newspaper Office.* Jonas' heart raced as the building grew closer.

He had a name now. Arthur Cutmore. From the look of his picture, he seemed rather well-to-do. Surely someone would know something about him. Jonas walked into the local newspaper office. A story. A business license. Charitable work. People like him were always doing something to get themselves in the paper. He reminded Jonas of Miller.

Miller was always doing things to get his name in print. Charity events. Donating his time to the children's ward of the hospital. Promoting local artists and small businesses. People in town all thought he did it out of kindness, but Jonas knew what he was really after. Notoriety. A pat on the back. New ways to show off how much better he was than everyone else.

This Arthur Cutmore looked like the same type.

The woman behind the counter smiled as Jonas walked up. "What can I do for you today?" she asked.

He slid the picture toward her. "I'm looking for anything you might be able to find on this man. Maybe a story about him."

"Is he a local?" she asked.

Jonas shook his head. "I don't think so."

"Hmm. May not be much available then. We don't usually report much outside of local events," she explained.

Jonas sighed.

The woman gave him a sympathetic smile. "Maybe we'll get lucky. If he's done anything noteworthy maybe news of it made its way here." She took the picture and read the name written at the bottom. "Arthur Cutmore..." She furrowed her brow. "Actually, I think we may have something."

"You know who he is?"

She shook her head. "No. But I'm certain I've heard that name before." She disappeared behind a large set of shelves and was gone for several minutes.

"Ah here it is." She came back holding a file folder in her hand. "I knew I'd heard that name before. Arthur Cutmore." She handed him a sheet of paper from the folder.

"What is this?"

"The missing person report. That's what you're here about, isn't it? Local businessman went missing a few months back. Arthur Cutmore."

"He's missing?"

"Oh yeah. Quite a mystery. Young, successful, admired. Rumor was, he started getting real reclusive. Stopped going to events. Stopped talking to his friends. Ignored his business. People hardly saw any sign of him for weeks. Then, one day, he just up and vanished. Poof. No trace of him."

So that was it. Arthur Cutmore disappeared. His father must have thought he ran off with Sally. That's why he attacked her.

"What about his parents?" Jonas asked. "How would I get in contact with them?"

"His parents? What do you mean?"

"They must have filed the report. How would someone contact them if they had information?"

She furrowed her brow and looked over the papers in the file. "No. No parents listed at all. Don't think he had any family. Only next of kin listed are a couple of friends. There's even a picture in the file of the three of them together."

She handed him the photograph. Three young men, dressed in fine clothing. It looked like they were standing in front of a shop. At the bottom of the picture it read, *Misters Cutmore, Portent, and Rose.*

"Certainly a handsome bunch," she smiled.

Jonas handed her back the picture and the missing person report. "Thank you for your help."

He walked out the door, unsure of what to do.

ARTHUR CUTMORE HAD something to do with all of this. Jonas could feel it. The man sneaking around Sally's, the handkerchief Abner found, the warnings to him and Miller. Cutmore or his father, maybe both of them. They were responsible for all of this.

As much as he hated the idea, he had to talk to Miller. He had to find out if he'd received anymore threats or seen anything suspicious.

The cold air outside burned his ears and nose as he walked down the street toward Miller's office. A stone path led up to the elaborately carved door. Jonas turned the knob, but found it still and firmly in place. Locked. Jonas checked his watch. A shabby second hand timepiece with a worn leather band.

10 am

Miller should have been there. Jonas peered in the windows, but he could see nothing but darkness inside. He could have been on a house call. Or maybe a meeting. Miller was on all kinds of boards and committees.

Jonas looked across the street at the bakery. Maeve always had an eye on things in the neighborhood. Especially things to do with Miller. Her window had a perfect view of his office. If anyone knew where Miller was, it would be her.

He walked into Maeve's, ushered in by the familiar chime of the little bell above the door. The warm smell of fresh bread filled his senses, washing over him. He forgot how much he loved that smell. He used to look forward to his trip to the bakery every morning. It was usually the best part of his day. But lately he'd stopped going. He tried to think of why, but didn't really have an answer. Just the normal busyness of life, he supposed.

Maeve stood behind the counter, kneading dough, sprinkling sugar. She was lost in the rhythm of the kitchen. Jonas watched her for a moment before she looked up and realized he was there.

"Jonas Decker!" Her eyes lit up, and she greeted him with a bright expression. "Why, I haven't seen you in so long I thought you'd dried up and blown away."

Jonas gave her a small chuckle. "Sorry, Maeve. Didn't mean to stay away so long. I've just had a lot going on."

"Spending all your time with that Sally, have you?" She gave him a coy grin.

Jonas nodded and smiled.

"Oh, she's a dear girl, isn't she?"

"I certainly think so," Jonas agreed.

"Well, good. You deserve a nice young lady in your life."

Jonas blushed a little.

"Well, now that I've got you here, what can I do for you?" she asked.

"I'm looking for Miller. I don't suppose you know where I'd find him?"

"Afraid I don't. I haven't seen the fine young doctor in days. Not a soul in or out of his door."

Jonas sighed and looked out the window at Miller's office.

"How about your usual?" Maeve said, handing him a small bundle wrapped in paper. "On the house."

Jonas unwrapped the pastry and bit into it. Warm, sweet, perfect. He'd forgotten how good Maeve's pastries were. Why hadn't he been showing up for breakfast? Now that he felt the warmth, tasted the soft fluffy bread melting on his tongue, he couldn't imagine missing a single breakfast.

"Folks in town were starting to fear you'd closed up shop," Maeve said, a worried tone to her normally chipper voice.

"Me?" Jonas asked between bites. "Why would anyone think that?"

"Lot of people have mentioned trying to get in and finding your pub door locked."

Jonas *had* been opening later and closing earlier recently, but he rarely had customers at those times. He supposed there had been a few days when he opted to help Sally at her shop instead of opening the pub. And she had been ill so often lately... she needed his help more and more. Maybe he had been neglecting the pub.

"Let everyone know I'm still open for business."

Maeve smiled. "Good to hear. Would hate to lose the pub. Such a nice little place you have."

Jonas nodded. It *was* a nice little place. He used to love it. Opening the pub in the morning was something he looked forward to. The people, the drinks, the atmosphere. But lately he just hadn't felt the same about it. Every time he looked around it seemed shabby, dingy, bleak. A lot of things in his life felt that way... but not everything. There were certain joys that remained untarnished by whatever mood he'd been in.

Things like Sally.

She was always a bright spot in his life. Even when everything else felt grim. Even when the things that used to bring him happiness just weren't working. He could always count on her. She always made him feel light and hopeful. But now that he was in a better mind about it, he really did need to take better care of the pub. He was a little ashamed to admit that he'd forgotten how much it meant to him. That was his business and his home. He loved it.

CHAPTER FOURTEEN
A Grim Warning

Jonas walked into the pub. The air inside was musty and stale from the door not being opened in days. He really had been neglecting it. He wiped down the counters of dust and took the chairs down off the tables.

Jonas gathered up the trash and stepped out the back door into the alley. A strong odor filled the air outside. Jonas pulled a face. With all the old meat and animal parts Gus had to throw out, it wasn't the first time his trash had been pungent. But this was certainly the worst it had ever been.

Jonas walked over to the bins and braced himself to see the source of the smell, but there was nothing there. Just an empty bin. No trash at all. Yet the smell of something rotten was still permeating the alley. It got stronger near Gus' door.

He knocked on the back door of the butcher shop. "Gus?" he called out. "Gus, I think something in your shop may have gone bad."

Jonas turned the knob. The door swung open with a creak. A strong smell emerged from the darkness, wafting out and hitting Jonas hard in the face.

He put his hand over his mouth and nose and grimaced at the foul stench. "What is that?"

The smell got stronger the further in he walked. A shiver of apprehension filled his body as he looked around. Tables, knives, cleavers. The tools of Gus' trade, still filthy from their last use. A heavy buzzing echoed from a table in the back. The air above it was black with flies.

There were also several wooden crates stacked in the back of the room. Jonas couldn't see what was in them, but something wet seemed to be oozing out of them.

His stomach turned as he walked through the shop. Red chunks of rotten meat covered the floor, writhing and wriggling with maggots. Gore and offal dripped down the sides of all the tables. Jonas retched and heaved.

"Gus?" He choked back another gag. "Gus, are you here somewhere?"

Jonas looked around the room, and something caught his eye. In the furthest corner, on the floor. Gus' apron... and something under it.

Jonas knealt down over the apron and lifted it up slowly. A skull, its withered skin pulled tight, thin and mummified. Its eyes dried and shriveled in their sockets. A look of horror on its face. *Gus.* There was no mistaking it. All that was left of him was his head. Jonas froze in place as he watched a small bit of Gus' face crumble and fall to the floor.

He tossed the apron hastily back over the skull. The smell from the room was wearing on him. His head was dizzy from trying not to breathe too deeply. Jonas coughed and gagged again, trying to prop himself up on Gus' desk.

He needed to get to the police. But he could barely stand up straight. His stomach rolled. He was going to be sick. There was a wastebasket under Gus' desk; Jonas pulled it toward him and hovered there until his head stopped spinning. All he could think of was getting out of that room. But something stopped him. A scrap of discarded paper in Gus' trash. A familiar warning scrawled in black ink.

Beware Sally Lockley.

Jonas looked back at the apron on the floor. Gus had gotten the same threatening note. And now he was dead. Someone was targeting Sally's suitors.

Jonas ran out the front door and down the street toward the police station.

JONAS STOOD OUTSIDE the butcher shop as the police examined what he'd found.

"Good news and bad," the officer said, stepping out of the shop. "Bad news is, I think you're right. It seems like it is Gus. Real shame. The good news is, no sign of foul play in the shop. Money was in the register and nothing was missing or disturbed. We won't know what happened until the coroner takes a look, but for now, it doesn't look like he was murdered or anything like that."

Jonas furrowed his brow. "No foul play? Most of his body was missing!"

The officer nodded. "I'm no doctor, but he looked like he'd been dead for a while. Seems like some animals may have gotten in and run off with most of the body. It's not typical, but I've seen it happen once or twice."

"What about the mess?" Jonas argued. "All that blood and gore?"

"Looks like he died before he had a chance to clean up for the night. Raw meat left out for a week or so, and..." The officer gestured towards the shop door. "That's about what I'd expect it to look and smell like."

Ugh. That smell. Even outside, Jonas couldn't escape it. Every time the door opened, another waft of putrid air escaped into the neighborhood.

The officer seemed sympathetic. "I know it looked like a crime scene in there. And you did the right thing coming to get us. But honestly, I don't think there's much mystery here." He sighed. "Gus lived on meat and ale, and took terrible care of himself. Sad as it is, it was probably natural causes. If the coroner says different, we'll investigate, but for now I don't think there's anything to find."

An older gentleman Jonas didn't recognize walked up the street toward them. He was small and wore a crumpled suit that seemed too large for him. He had thick glasses and a gray patchy beard.

"Good. Coroner's here," the officer said, pointing towards the shop door. "He's right inside there, Sulley. Not much left of him to collect."

"Wait, Sulley?" Jonas asked. "Where's Miller? I thought he was the coroner?"

"Oh, you didn't hear?"

Jonas shook his head.

"On a call out of town. Some well-to-do patient, specifically wanted Dr. Miller to tend to them. Must have paid him a fortune to get him to close up his office and tend to just one soul. He had to leave quickly, too. Guess he'll be gone for a while."

"When did he leave?" Jonas asked.

"Bout a week or so ago. Just took off one afternoon after a house call. His nurse stopped by the station to tell us we'd need to find a replacement for a while."

"He didn't tell you himself?"

The officer shook his head. "Didn't tell anyone. His nurse was as surprised as we were. Said he went out on a house call one afternoon and didn't come back. Next morning she came in to a note on her desk telling her he'd be out of town. We've got ol' Sulley there, taking over for him while he's gone."

The older gentleman came out of the butcher shop holding a large tray with a small sheet over it. His brow was deeply furrowed, and he looked confused. "I... I've never seen anything like it..."

The officer looked concerned. "What is it, Sulley?"

"Fell to pieces," Sulley muttered. "It just fell to pieces when I tried to put it on the tray...Not even *pieces*, more like... *dust*."

"What did?" the officer asked. But Jonas already knew. He'd seen it happen, too.

"Gus' head," Sulley looked bewildered. "It just turned to dust."

Sully wandered away with the tray in his hands, still muttering as he left.

Jonas raised an eyebrow. "Nothing to investigate?"

The officer rolled his eyes. "I'll give it to you; that was odd. But so far, it's still not criminal."

Jonas shook his head, frustrated, and walked away from the butcher shop. The smell was still lingering in the air, and he'd had all he could stand of it. He headed back toward his pub. An ominous feeling crept over him, like walking through spiderwebs but not knowing where the spider was. Something wasn't right. The police may not have wanted to see it, but it was there. Something menacing. Jonas could feel it.

Three men in the neighborhood were all threatened; warned to stay away from Sally. Abner had seen someone sneaking around her building in the middle of the night. What if Sally was in danger?

Whoever this person was, they clearly wanted her all to themselves. Was it some hidden admirer? Someone from her past, maybe?

A sickening thought gnawed at the back of Jonas' mind. *That locket.* That gold flower locket. She wore it every day. She *clung* to it so tightly. What if the man inside it still clung to her just as tightly? What if he was the man sending the threatening notes?

The police didn't believe that Gus was murdered, but Jonas wasn't convinced. And if he *was* murdered, the killer's face could be hidden in that locket. *That ridiculous locket.* Why was she so protective of it? So protective of *him*?

Whoever he was.

It drove Jonas mad. But there was nothing he could do about it. If he pressed it any further, he'd only drive her away. He was determined not to do that. But he had to do something.

CHAPTER FIFTEEN
The Weary Nurse

Jonas walked down the street, moving away from the crowd that had formed around Gus' shop. He needed a quiet place to think. The police weren't taking him seriously, but he knew that note had something to do with Gus' death. It was too much of a coincidence. They'd all been warned to stay away from Sally.

Jonas wondered if that's why Miller had been so quick to leave town. Maybe he'd been warned again. Or threatened in some other way. Jonas couldn't exactly ask him, he didn't even know where Miller was.

But there was someone who might.

Clara.

If anyone knew where Miller had gone, it would be Clara. His nurse, his closest friend, and the only person he told he was leaving. He might have even told her if he was being threatened.

Jonas needed to talk to her. If she had any information, he needed to find out. For Gus. For Sally. For all of them.

Clara lived in a little cottage on the farthest edge of the neighborhood. It was mid-afternoon. She was usually looking after the office at this time. But with Miller away, she'd almost certainly be home.

Jonas walked up the little path to Clara's house. It was lined with hedges of camellia and winter jasmine. Their smell perfumed the air; sweet and luxurious, but soft and welcoming. He'd grown so used to the thick, overpowering scents of Sally's shop, drenching the humid air with saccharin. He'd forgotten how nice it could be to smell something light and fresh out in the world. The delicate scent drifted on the breeze, fluttering through the crisp winter air.

He would have thought, having just found a body, it would be impossible to relax. But something about Clara's garden and the wide open air was oddly peaceful, despite it all. There was a calmness here that stripped away the noise and clutter filling his head.

Jonas found himself lost in it all for a moment. The gentle beauty. The quiet. It felt like the first time his mind had been quiet in weeks. With so much going on, he hadn't noticed how loud and intrusive his thoughts had been until they were silent.

As the dirt path slowly turned into stepping stones beneath his feet, he saw Clara's front door open.

"Jonas?" She beamed at him from the doorway. Her smile was beautiful. "Come in."

CLARA'S HOME WAS SMALL, but cozy. A fire was burning in the hearth and the smell of fresh bread filled the air. On the wall was a framed tintype; Clara with Jonas and Miller. He furrowed his brow and looked closer. Jonas couldn't remember ever having a picture taken with Miller, but there it was.

He leaned in closer, examining every detail. Clara was in front, looking beautiful as always. He and Miller were behind her. He stared at the image of himself. It was like looking at a stranger.

"The fairgrounds last year," Clara smiled. "A man there had a little booth and was making pictures. You remember?"

Jonas stared at the picture. "I... I remember the fairgrounds." He shook his head. "But not the picture." In honesty, until she said it, he hadn't even remembered the fair. Jonas only vaguely remembered being there with Clara. He certainly didn't remember Miller being with them. He couldn't imagine himself spending that much time with him. Maybe that was why he'd pushed it from his memory.

"I can't believe you don't remember," Clara laughed. "Miller and I practically had to drag you over to the booth. You're so camera-shy. I think none of us would have a single picture of you if we didn't force you to take one with us."

It was true, Jonas wasn't especially fond of pictures. He didn't have any at all of himself. Something about looking at his own image in a frame just didn't sit right in his eyes. Probably because he never liked how he looked in them. Though he had to admit, the one on Clara's wall wasn't terrible.

He sat with Clara and she smiled fondly at him from across the small table. The sun beamed through the window, dancing across the room in bright slivers of light. She handed him a warm cup trimmed in gold and filled with fresh tea. It was smooth and citrus-y with just a hint of sugar. The taste hit his tongue and spread like a wave of comfort through his entire body. At that moment, it was the most delicious thing he could remember tasting.

He wasn't sure what it was about Clara's house, but somehow everything seemed unclouded and vibrant. Clearer. Like a web of noise and anxiety had been lifted from his mind.

"It's been far too long since you've been by. Since anyone's been by, really. Dr. Miller is the only one who ever visits. And he's been out of town with a patient." She kept her tone light, but there was a quiet sadness behind her voice.

"Speaking of Miller, have you heard from him since he left?" Jonas asked.

Clara shook her head. She seemed troubled at the mention of his absence. "He's been away for weeks now, without a word."

"Where is he, exactly?"

She gave a small shrug and a quiet sniffle. "I wish I knew. He never said where he was going. No contact information at all. He didn't even say goodbye. Just a note on my desk."

"Had anything unusual happened before he left? Odd correspondence? Maybe someone said or did something that might have upset him?"

Clara furrowed her brow. "What do you mean?"

"Had anyone threatened him?"

"Who would threaten Dr. Miller? Everyone loves him." She paused for a moment. "Oh... you mean *that note*? The one warning him away from that strange woman with the plants?"

Jonas nodded. "Had he received any more of those?"

"No. He said he knew who sent it, and it was nothing to worry about." But she did look worried. "Was he wrong?"

"I got a similar warning written on my pub window. And Gus at the butcher shop got a note like Miller's." He was reluctant to say more, but he knew he had to. "The thing is... Gus. He's..."

"He's what?"

"Dead."

"*Dead*?" Clara gasped. "What happened?"

"I'm not sure. The police are insisting it was natural causes, but I found the body and that note in his trash and-" Jonas sighed. "I just wanted to see if Miller could shed anymore light on it."

"He mentioned the note the morning he left. That's when he said everything was fine now. But that's all he said. Then, that afternoon, he went out on that house call. He said it was for you."

"It wasn't for me, exactly. It was for Sally Lockley."

"That's the woman with the plants?" Clara's jaw seemed to tense a little.

Jonas nodded. "She'd been ill and asked if I could get Miller for her. He came by that afternoon and gave her a tonic that seemed to help. She said he left abruptly."

"Jonas, this isn't like him. He wouldn't just abandon his practice and all his patients."

Jonas sighed. Clara was right. It did seem out of character for Miller to just disappear. "What did the note he left for you say?"

Clara walked over to a small desk in the corner and pulled a slip of paper from one of the drawers. She handed it to Jonas.

Clara-

A patient is in need of my care. I'll be away for quite some time. I'll explain when I return.

Try not to worry.

Miller

The note held little in the way of clues. He obviously didn't want anyone to know where he was going.

"But if he were going to care for a patient and was closing the office anyway, why not take you along to help him? You're his nurse."

Clara shook her head. "I've been wondering the same thing."

"Had anyone new come into the office?"

"I don't think-"She furrowed her brow. "Actually, yes. That morning. A handsome, well-dressed man came into the office. He didn't give his name. He just said he needed to speak to Dr. Miller.

That it was urgent. I didn't hear what they spoke about; they went outside. I didn't see him again after that."

"Did he have a rose embroidered on his lapel?"

"Yes!" Clara shrieked excitedly. "You saw him?"

"Just for a moment. When they were talking outside. Do you think that's who gave Miller the job?"

"It has to be. Dr. Miller doesn't have any existing patients out of town. But he didn't leave his name or any information."

Jonas hated to admit it, but he was also starting to worry about Miller. It was all so strange. Disappearing the way he did, a patient no one had ever met, leaving Clara behind. Nothing about it made sense.

"That's probably the only person in the world who knows where Dr. Miller is." There was a small crackle of concern in her voice. She stared up at him with her large brown eyes.

Jonas took her hand in his. "Don't worry, Clara. We'll find him. I did see that man one other time out in front of my pub. If I see him again, I'll talk to him. I'll find out where Miller is. I promise."

Clara smiled. She had a beautiful smile.

CHAPTER SIXTEEN
Plant Food

It was a strange few days for Jonas, after finding Gus' body. Most of the neighborhood still didn't know he was dead. The police were still investigating and hadn't released any information yet. Only the neighbors on their block knew anything was wrong.

Jonas had sworn to himself that he'd keep his pub open, and he wanted to. But knowing there might be some madman out there obsessed with Sally, threatening her suiters, maybe even killing? He couldn't leave her alone. The pub could wait a few more days, just until the police had checked into Gus' death.

And it wasn't all bad. It meant spending more time with Sally. Company well spent as far as Jonas was concerned. He told her about Gus' death, but he didn't dare mention the note in his trash or the threats he and Miller had received. There was no need to worry her. She had enough on her mind just trying to keep her poor plants healthy.

Sally ran her hand across a wilting leaf and sighed.

"Are they hungry again?" Jonas asked.

She nodded.

"So soon? It feels like you just fed them."

"I know. But it wasn't enough. My poor plants can't live on the few bugs that make their way into the shop. I've tried leaving out fruit and such to attract more, but I just can't collect enough to keep them all nourished."

"What about that special powder you used on them?" Jonas asked. "That always seems to do the trick."

"Oh, it does. But it's so hard to get." She gave him a mischievous smile. "I've had another idea, though." She took him by the hand and led him down the long hallway in the back of the shop. A single door sat at the end; a heavy chain and padlock wrapped ominously across it. He'd always assumed it led out to the alley, but he was beginning to doubt that now.

Jonas hesitated. "What's all this, Sally?"

"I know it looks a bit strange, but I didn't want a customer accidentally walking in."

"Walking into *what*?"

She pulled out a key and unlocked the padlock. The chains fell away with a loud, unsettling rattle.

That smell.

That foul, reeking smell of rot and death. It was like being back in the butcher shop. Jonas took a step backward. His eyes began to water and his stomach turned.

Sally crinkled her nose. "I know it's a bit much." She walked into the darkness and turned on a lantern on the wall. She motioned for him to follow her. "Come see."

It was a small room, little more than a closet, really. It had a stack of wooden crates near the far wall. The light in that corner was dim, and Jonas couldn't see what was in them.

There was a table in the back with a small grinder in the center. A metal drum was positioned nearby.

He walked closer to the grinder, choking on the stench filled air. The table was stained red, coated in sticky puddles of blood and matter. The grinder atop it was covered in thick red grime. He peered into its gaping maw. Rows of metal teeth and gears, bits of bone and rotten flesh still stuck between them.

He gagged again, and his eyes began to water.

He plucked a bloody chunk of hair from the grinder and stared at it in disbelief.

Jonas looked into the metal drum next to the table. Festering pieces of muscle and tissue floated and bobbed their way through the liquid. Sally dipped her hand into it and pulled out a handful of its contents.

"I'm making my own plant food for them," she said proudly.

The blood trickled down her slender arm. A stain of red across her soft, pale skin. She smiled, beaming with pride over her creation. "This will keep the plants fed for weeks. Maybe months if I can keep getting a hold of scraps to add to the broth."

The scattered chunks of rotten meat and puddles of blood cast an eerie red glow to the light in the room. Jonas wasn't sure why, but it somehow made Sally even more beautiful. He stood staring at her for a moment, lost in her image, until the mixture in the vat gurgled, letting out new and horrible smells.

The stench jarred him back to reality, and he gagged again.

She smiled and rolled her eyes. "Oh, it's not all that bad. The smell certainly takes some getting used to and I'm sure you understand now why I can't have customers wondering in. But it will keep the plants healthy for so much longer."

"Sally, *what is that*?" he asked again, staring at her bloody hand.

"I know it looks terrible, but it's just a bit of leftover meat."

"Meat?"

"When you told me about the mess at Gus' shop, I realized how much good it could do for my plants. I wanted to put it to some use. He had all kinds of things, just spoiling and going to waste. It was a shame, really."

"So you just gathered it up and brought it all over here?"

"Oh, his landlord was happy for me to do it." She assured him. "Much less cleanup for him."

Jonas looked over at a shelf with half a dozen plants on it. Despite receiving no light within the small, dark room, they were large and thriving. Huge, bloody red veins ran beneath their green skin, pulsating and throbbing as the plants writhed and wriggled in their pots. Blood dripped from their spines, and chunks of meat were wrapped in the barbs of their vines. They looked different from the plants in the storefront. Violent. Menacing.

"Are these Gus' plants?"

"Oh, yes. I couldn't just leave the poor dears there to starve. But, they've been living on raw meat at Gus' shop for so long... it's made them look a bit *different*. I thought it might be best to keep them back here instead of out front. Customers coming into the shop wouldn't understand them the way I do."

Jonas walked closer to one of the plants and it seemed to lunge at him. They'd certainly become more dangerous. It was odd, Jonas didn't remember seeing the plants anywhere when he'd found Gus' body. Just rotten meat everywhere.

"So all of this is just the leftovers from the butcher shop?" Jonas asked.

"Well..." She swirled her hand around in the vat. "Not all of it."

Jonas furrowed his brow.

"Gus only had so much meat in his shop. And there's not another butcher on this side of town. So, to keep the mixture full, I did have to get a bit creative." Her eyes flickered briefly to the wooden crates behind him.

Jonas was closer to the crates now. The light was still dim, but he could see them more clearly. He peered inside.

Rat traps. Dozens and dozens of rat traps. All empty.

Jonas looked at the bloody chunk of hair, still gripped between his fingers. He dropped it onto the floor and shivered.

Sally stirred the vat with her delicate fingers, gently swirling the putrid stew. It spit out another burst of rotten stench into the air. The smell hit Jonas' senses, and he pulled his eyes away from Sally. He coughed and felt his stomach flip. Queasy and dizzy from the stale air of the small windowless room, he coughed again. "Sally? Could we..." Jonas motioned at the door for them to leave.

Sally wiped the blood and gore from her hand and onto a small towel. She smiled and led him out of the room, seeming to take pity on him. She closed the door and relocked the chains and padlock that spread across it.

"If you're going to be any use to me, we're going to have to strengthen your constitution," she teased. "I need you at your best."

He smiled. He wasn't sure he'd ever be able to get used to a smell like that, but he did like that Sally wanted him to be more involved in her life.

CHAPTER SEVENTEEN
The Locket

It took over a week, but Gus' death was finally reported in the paper.

A tragic loss.

Friend and neighbor, gone too soon.

Natural causes.

Jonas sighed. Nothing about it felt *natural* to him. But no one would listen. The only person who might believe him was Miller. But he still wasn't back yet. Off in another town, tending to a patient as a private physician. Probably making a fortune. Meanwhile, everything in their own town was falling apart. Abner was gone. Gus was gone, and with him went the butcher shop. Jonas hadn't opened his own pub in days.

And worst of all, Sally was ill again.

Sweet Sally. Pale and weak. The illness left her drained and bound to her bed. All Jonas could do was watch over her and help keep her shop running as best he could. It was still the early hours of the day, barely six in the morning, but Jonas unlocked the plant shop door and put the open sign in the window.

Might as well get an early start.

He looked out the window into the thick fog of morning. It hung heavy in the street, but Jonas could make out his pub standing stoic across the way. And there was something else. Something pacing the mist. A man. He was standing outside the pub, walking back and forth in front of the door. *Who would be out so early?*

Jonas leaned closer to the glass and squinted his eyes, trying to get a better look at the figure. The fog parted for just a moment, and Jonas recognized him. *The man with the rose embroidered on his lapel.*

His heart raced. He needed to talk to him. To find out where Miller was. Clara would finally have some answers. She'd been so worried. Jonas started out the door, his hand on the knob, but stopped.

Something pulled at him; a racing feeling through his veins. It trembled through his body. It scratched at the back of his mind.

He pulled his hand away from the doorknob. He needed to be *here*. Sally needed him to be *here*. What if she got worse?

No. He couldn't leave. Miller was fine. He was always fine. Sally was the one who was ill. She was the one who needed help. Miller was off with a patient somewhere.

Though he had made a promise to Clara... He remembered the sadness in her voice. The tiny sniffles as she spoke. Her large brown eyes staring at him, hoping for answers about where her friend had gone. Jonas reached for the doorknob again. Maybe he could spare a moment to talk to the man. Just to ease Clara's mind. She was so worried about Miller. Though Jonas couldn't imagine why.

What had Miller ever done to deserve such devotion? Even now, he'd disappeared without any consideration for her and still she worried after him. Why did a man like that have *so much*? Why did Clara care *so much*? It was infuriating.

Jonas' face hardened, and he pulled his hand away from the door. *No.*

If Clara was going to be so easily taken in by Miller's charms, there was nothing Jonas could do for her.

But Sally...

Sally wouldn't be fooled by a money clip and a handsome face. She didn't care about status. Sally was who he owed his time to.

Jonas didn't want Clara to worry, but it was her own fault for caring so much about a man like that.

Jonas was where he needed to be. He turned from the door and stepped away. The anxious scratching in his mind faded. Jonas sighed, relieved. He was making the right choice. *Sally* was the right choice.

JONAS WALKED UP THE stairs to Sally's room and peeked in the doorway to check on her. She was still sleeping. A tangle of dark curls fell across her pillow. Dark circles beneath her eyes hung heavy in the shadows of the room. And the locket draped across her chest, rising and falling with her breath. He caught his jaw tightening as he watched the pale sliver of dawn gleam off its polished golden surface. *That ridiculous locket.* His teeth ground against each other in his mouth as he stared at it. It wasn't just a locket. Not really. Not to Jonas. It was another man's face. Another man laying draped across her heart.

The thought whirred through his mind. It had weighed on him for weeks. But something about seeing her there, so frail and helpless, made the thought weigh all the heavier. The man in that locket wasn't caring for her. He wasn't standing vigil at her side. He didn't deserve to keep such a hold on her heart.

Jonas pushed the thought from his mind. No. It was her past to hold on to. It was her love to remember. He had no right to demand she remove her past from sight. He knew it was true, but the bitterness still plagued him. The jealousy of some unknown figure darkening their life from within a piece of jewelry. It wasn't even the locket that drove him mad... it was not knowing who was hiding himself away in there. What face was locked behind the gold etched flower? If he just knew what the man looked like. Maybe that would be enough. He'd asked before, and she'd refused to tell him anything. But she was asleep now...

He crept toward her bedside, eyes fixed on the heaving gold locket. She lay there, eyes tight, body limp. *Just a peek.* If he could just open the locket as she slept, he'd be able to see inside, and Sally would never be the wiser. He felt silly in his desperation, but even knowing how childish it was, he could not stop himself.

Jonas reached for the locket. He'd only planned to look inside, but the chain had come unclasped as she slept and the locket slipped from her neck. It practically leapt into his hand. He stood frozen, staring at the necklace he now held. Sally stirred in her bed, letting out a soft sigh and rolling over in her bedding.

Jonas waited for her to settle, then raced downstairs and hid himself away in the storeroom behind the shop counter. She'd wake any moment and realize the locket was missing. He'd never convince her it came unfastened on its own, not after the fuss he'd made about knowing who was inside.

He moved toward the window to use the early morning light. It was still the milky twilight of dawn, but the rising sunlight was bright enough to see the locket clearly. He dug his fingers into the seam and pried it open. It was tight, but it relented with a soft click. Now he'd finally see. He'd know the face of the man she treasured.

Its secrets were no more. Jonas stared down at the locket, expecting the handsome face of Sally's past love. But what met his eyes was frightful. A ghastly nightmare stared back at him. A twisted, rotting face peered out from the frame. Sunken cheeks, straggles of patchy hair, pale flesh peeling from its bones. Its milky eyes stared wildly out at him. The creature's jaw hung slack in a silent scream.

Jonas gasped and tossed the locket, still open, onto the floor. He felt suddenly ill and weak. He stumbled, crashing hard into a shelf of potted plants, catching himself on a nearby table. Fear and horror spread through his body as he looked down at his own shriveled arms. His hands were gnarled, his skin dry and pale. He forced himself toward the mirror on the wall. His gaunt, withered face stared back at him.

Jonas screamed at the sight of himself. But the voice that left him was faint and raspy. He watched his reflection as it aged and decayed before his eyes. Lips and gums receding, forcing his face into a painful, skeletal smile. His hair fell out in clumps, leaving scraggly patches across his scalp. His muscles began to weaken and atrophy, causing him to fall to the floor.

Jonas lay there, staring at the open locket, just out of reach. He tried to crawl toward it. He didn't know what was happening, but something kept echoing in his mind.

I need to close the locket.

He didn't know why, but something told him he needed to close that locket. A fleeting memory, a vague echo in his mind. He'd heard the phrase before. The old man screamed it in his face after attacking Sally. *It must stay closed.* Jonas didn't know what it meant, but it was the only thought that surfaced in his mind as he saw the locket laying on the storeroom floor. Over and over again. *It must stay closed.*

Jonas dug his fingers into the floor and pulled himself forward with all the strength he had left. He inched his way toward the locket. Weak. Gasping. Fingernails bloody and aching. He forced his shriveled arm to extend, reaching out. He almost had it.

"What on earth is going on down here?" Sally's voice called out from the doorway.

He stared up at her. He tried to speak but could only manage to moan out a few low, guttural sounds.

Sally gasped. "What are you doing on the floor?" She raced toward him. Jonas reached out for her, but she ignored him. Scooping up the locket in her hands instead. She slipped it around her neck and fastened the clasp.

Sally sighed with a long deep breath, then smiled down at Jonas. She didn't look ill anymore. She looked radiant. Her skin was aglow, no longer pale or sallow. Her eyes were back to their vibrant, enchanting green. No sign of age or illness.

Jonas stared up at her. His body decayed and crumbling away. The locket around her neck was still open. The picture was no longer the horrifying corpse-like creature he'd seen inside. It was a man. Young, strong, healthy. *It was him*. The picture in the locket was Jonas. It smiled out from the frame. A wide, sinister grin.

That grin. That horrible, mocking grin. It was the last thing Jonas saw as his eyes dried and his body turned to dust.

CHAPTER EIGHTEEN
Sally Lockley

Sally snapped the locket closed and smiled down fondly at its shiny gold visage. The flower on the surface gleamed happily. A surge of energy and vitality was coursing through her. Her whole body felt light. She hadn't felt this good in months... not since Cutmore ruined everything for her.

She'd worked so hard on Arthur Cutmore. Luring him in. Separating him from everyone else in his life. Filling his head with whispers of doubt and jealousy.

He thought only of her.

He looked only at her.

He spoke only of her.

Until he was fat... dripping with love and desire. It was perfect. Only for him to close the locket and escape before she'd had her fill. Now he was out there, alive. He knew her secret. He knew her face. She hadn't thought it would be a problem at first. He didn't much look like himself anymore. Once he'd opened the locket, it drained the youth and vigor from his body. And his story would certainly have been taken as the ravings of a madman.

That's what she thought, anyway...

But within days, she began hearing rumors. Her name in connection with his disappearance. Whispers that someone was looking for her. She had no choice but to leave the bustling city she loved and run off to hide away in this tiny little village.

It'd been nothing but bad luck since then. It seemed there were no quality meals in this little town. A fishmonger. An old drunk. *Scraps.*

She nearly had the doctor, she was certain of it. All that flirting. All that time. She still didn't understand why he wouldn't take the bait. She put the locket right in his hand, but he wouldn't open it. He just gave her an odd look and handed her a tonic from his bag. It was like he *knew.* But he couldn't have.

She had to resort to making time with that boorish butcher, just to sustain herself.

But *Jonas,* he was something special. He was a meal she could live off of for months. All that affection. All that attention. And that sweet, mouth-watering rivalry she'd stirred up between him and the doctor. Sally took a deep breath and savored the feelings rushing through her. *Delicious.*

It was a shame, though. He'd been so helpful around the shop. Moving things, tidying up, he was quite good at all that. She could especially use that now. She looked around at the disarray surrounding her.

Jonas had left her shop in quite a mess. Broken glass, toppled plants, a pile of bone dust strewn across the floor. Tiny particles of dry skin and hair floated through the air, catching in the beams of morning sunlight.

Sally sighed and opened the empty metal canister on the nearby shelf. "Can't waste good plant food." She grabbed the broom and dustpan that were leaned against the wall. But she was interrupted by the gentle ring of a bell.

The front door.

Her heart raced, and she panicked briefly. Someone was in the shop. What if they were here to see Jonas? What if they came into the back and saw the pile of dust and withered bits of skin? Would they realize it was him? She took a deep breath. It was fine. She'd done this before. She pulled a crate of pots in front of what was left of Jonas to keep him out of sight and quickly made her way to the front room.

"I'm sorry, we're not o-" She stopped in her tracks. "Oh. Hello."

"I apologize, ma'am," the man said with a smile. He was strong and handsome. An intriguing duality emanated from him; naive, yet sophisticated. Sweetness wrapped in debonair. He smelled of expensive aftershave and wore a custom suit with a small rose embroidered on the lapel. "Should I come back after while?" he asked.

Sally felt the locket stir at the sight of him. A rumble penetrated deep into her chest. A hunger bloomed inside her as she stared into his crystal blue eyes. "No, no. Don't be silly," she said with a breathless smile. "I'd be delighted to help you."

The man reached out a hand to greet her. "Desmond Rose."

Rose... what a lovely name.

She took his hand. The locket quivered with anticipation. "Sally Lockley." His touch made her whole body tingle. A hunger riled by the scent of this intoxicating man.

"I've just bought a place here in town, and the front garden is a bit of a wreck. I'd like to fix it up, but I'm afraid I don't know much about plants."

Sally smiled. It was a kind, warm smile, never betraying a hint of malice. She'd perfected it over the years. "Not to worry Mr. Rose. You've come to exactly the right place."

She was using her sweetest voice, her kindest smile, her most adoring visage. But Mr. Rose seemed distracted. He was staring out the window.

"Is something the matter?"

"Not at all," he said, pulling his eyes away from the window and meeting Sally's gaze. "I just... I don't suppose you know when that place across the street opens, do you? I've tried stopping by a couple of days in a row, but no matter the time of day, it never seems to be open." He gestured towards Jonas' pub.

"Oh," Sally said. "That would be Jonas Decker's pub."

Mr. Rose perked up. "So you know him, then? Do you know when he'll be there? I'm fairly new in town; I thought it might be a good place to meet the neighbors."

Sally cast her eyes down, feigning a look of sadness. "Unfortunately, Jonas- Mr. Decker, I mean, is no longer in the neighborhood. He left town quite recently."

Mr. Rose looked disappointed. "That's a real shame. I'd really hoped to meet him."

"Oh, he was a lovely man. He helped me through some difficult times. Sadly, he wasn't much of a businessman. He just couldn't seem to keep the pub going. Most days, he didn't even bother opening it."

Mr. Rose looked sympathetic. "It can be difficult. I assume having such a lovely and distracting neighbor in you didn't help him any." He flashed a dashing smile.

Sally blushed. "And what is it that you do, Mr. Rose? Do you have your own business?"

"Oh, no." Mr. Rose shook his head. "Not much of a head for business, myself." He had a slight southern accent, but she couldn't identify the region. "I travel, mostly. Gathering up items for a little shop."

"Fascinating." Sally reveled in her luck. She loved a man who traveled for a living. They were almost never reported missing. No policemen poking around. No questions to answer.

She walked him toward a wall of plants. "Tell me, Mr. Rose, what's brought you to our sleepy little town? Do you have family here?"

He smiled. It was a sweet, bashful kind of smile. "No, nothing like that. I don't really know anyone here. And I haven't got much in the way of family."

No connections to sever. She wouldn't even have to isolate him from friends and family; he'd already done half her work for her. No roots. No friendships. No ties to unbind. He was perfect.

Though it still wasn't going to be easy. Mr. Rose had a quiet confidence about him. Confidence was always a bit difficult to break. That's likely where she went wrong with Dr. Miller. That man's self assurance was virtually unshakable.

But Mr. Rose would be different. She'd devote all of her attention to him. Ignore everyone else. It would take every ounce of her energy, use up everything she'd gained from Jonas, but it would be worth it. Something about Mr. Rose radiated with delicious vitality. Sweet, juicy, practically pouring off of him with each smile or flutter of his eyes in her direction.

He really was quite attractive. Fair, with a kiss of sun to his skin. Like he was from somewhere much warmer. Sandy brown hair. Eyes a shade of blue she'd never seen before. He'd look lovely in her locket. And he seemed like pleasant company as well. She really wouldn't mind taking the time to wear at his confidence. Fill him full of doubt and dependency on her. Though she did wish he'd stop asking about Jonas.

He looked back out the window toward the pub. "So the two of you were close?" he asked.

Sally smiled sadly. "We were for a time." She felt the locket shiver again. "He was a good friend and always such a help around the shop. And he took such good care of me."

"How do you mean?" Mr. Rose asked.

"I was very ill recently and Jonas nursed me back to health. I don't know what I'll do now that he's gone."

"Well, I don't know much about illness or medicine," Mr. Rose began, "but I do have quite a lot of free time these days. So if you ever need anything, I'm happy to oblige."

Sally beamed brightly. "That's a lovely offer, Mr. Rose. I believe I'll take you up on that."

He let out a small sigh of relief. "Good to hear. I was afraid that might have been a bit forward. With your friend just leaving and all."

"Jonas Decker was the past," she said. "Right now, I'm much more interested in the future. And I think helping you with your garden is exactly what my future needs."

Mr. Rose smiled. "I couldn't agree more."

CHAPTER NINETEEN

The Parlor

The grandfather clock ticked and tocked in its own odd, unsettling rhythm. It chimed occasionally, though never on the hour.

Surely it was broken.

And yet it stood prominently in the dimly lit parlor. The only timepiece in the room. The only way for anyone to track the passage of the day. This large, broken clock.

A finely dressed man paced the floor, feet filled with worry. The clock clicked away in perfect sync with his footsteps. At this point, he wasn't certain if he was pacing to match its rhythm or if its rhythm had changed to suit his steps. He stopped near the couch. The ticking sound faltered for just a moment as he did. Perhaps the clock wasn't broken after all; just mocking him.

Dr. Miller sat down on the overstuffed sofa, sinking into its red velvet cushions. He stared down at his tea, sitting cold on the table. A red floral pattern wrapped its way around the cup. He sighed.

Weeks.

He'd been here for weeks. Or was it months? He wasn't entirely certain anymore.

It wasn't that he disliked the room. It was lovely and comfortable. But he'd grown weary. Weary of the waiting. And of being cooped up, unable to leave. More than anything, he was bored. Nothing irritated him more than having nothing to do.

His practice, his patients, meetings, charity events. His days were usually full. But these last few weeks had been quiet. And lonely. Left in a plush parlor, waiting on the word of a man he hardly knew, but somehow trusted.

His mind flashed back to that day.

"She feeds on men. Drains their life and turns their bones to dust."

Miller likely wouldn't have listened to the man at all had it not been for that last bit. *Bones to dust.* The state he'd found poor Abner in. He couldn't explain it. Medicine couldn't explain it. But Desmond Rose had an answer. It was unbelievable. Like the rantings of a madman. But it *was* an answer.

"She needs you to open the locket," Rose said. "That's the only way she can feed. She'll try to convince you to do it, but you can't. If you want to survive, it must stay closed." His words were nonsense, but his tone was so serious Miller found himself compelled to listen.

Miller wasn't sure what to think of it all. Until an ill and frail Sally put the locket in his hands.

"I'd like to look at the picture inside, but I'm too weak to open the clasp. Could you open it for me?"

Mr. Rose's words rushed back into Miller's mind, echoing in his ears. *It must stay closed.*

He dropped the locket and left as quickly as he could. He ran into Rose as soon as he walked out the door. Miller barely had time to leave a note on Clara's desk before Rose led him down a foggy alley and out of Sally's grasp.

He'd been here ever since. Though he wasn't entirely sure where *here* was.

Miller sat on the couch, eyes fixed on his teacup. If only he had something to do. Something to focus his mind on. A patient to cure. An illness to identify. At least when Rose was in the house, he had someone to talk to. But Rose left weeks earlier, promising that when he got back Sally would be dealt with.

Dealt with? What did that mean?

What if he couldn't deal with her? What if she got him instead?

The clock made another strained chime. Miller glared in its direction. One more day alone with nothing to do and he was taking that thing apart.

He barely had time to think the threat when a new sound caught his attention.

The front door.

It hadn't opened in weeks. Miller turned toward the door with anticipation. A man walked in and took off his top hat, revealing the short, sandy brown hair beneath. He hung his hat on the nearby rack and walked into the parlor.

He was impeccably dressed. His suit had a small rose embroidered on the lapel.

Miller looked at him expectantly, but he said nothing.

The man pulled the top from a large decanter; it loosened with a loud pop. He poured the brown liquid into a small glass and took a long sip.

"Is it over?" Miller asked. "Good lord, Rose, say something."

Mr. Rose tossed a gold flower locket onto the coffee table. It was wide open.

Miller took a step away from it. "I thought we weren't supposed to open it."

Mr. Rose smiled. "I reckon that locket's likely had its last meal, at least for a while. Thought you might want to see for yourself."

Miller took a step toward the table and peered at the picture in the locket. A dark-haired woman with fair skin and deep green eyes. *It was Sally.* Her face was twisted into a horrifying scream. Vicious. Ravenous. A look of terror and rage.

"Sally? How? What happened?"

"She needed me to open the locket. Needed to feed." Rose smiled. The southern in his voice was more pronounced than usual. "But she found I'm not such easy prey to catch. She looked for someone else to open it, but this town's a small one, and I reckon she'd run out of options before she was too weak to sort herself. It had to be me. And that certainly wasn't going to happen. Longer I refused, weaker she got. 'Til the fight went right out of her. You've seen it? The way her body and health deteriorate?"

Miller nodded.

"She was being drained into her own trap. Eating herself alive 'til all that remained was a gold flower locket... and dust. Found the locket, wide open on her bed. That picture screaming from inside." Rose walked over to the table and picked up the locket. "Her due's finally come." He snapped the locket closed and placed it back on the table. "Suits her, far as I'm concerned."

Miller sat back down on the sofa. He didn't understand most of what was happening. But he trusted Desmond Rose. Miller stared at the locket.

"I still wouldn't open it if I were you," Rose warned. "Just to be on the safe side."

Miller nodded. He had no interest in ever seeing inside that cursed thing again. He sat silent for a moment, his mind racing. It wasn't that he didn't have any questions, more that he had too many questions.

Rose took another sip from his glass. "Spoke to your gal, Clara. She's awful worried about you, but I let her know you were doing just fine."

Miller closed his eyes and sighed. *Clara.* "What did you tell her?"

"Told her I brought you on as a private physician. Said I had a friend that needed help, couldn't leave the house. That leaving would be dangerous for him." Rose shrugged. "Wasn't exactly a lie. Just didn't mention that *you* were the friend."

Miller gave him a skeptical smile. "And did she accept that answer?"

"'Course not. But not much she could say without kicking up a fuss."

Miller noticed Rose's accent thickened whenever he was tired or under significant stress. He couldn't be certain which was bringing out the drawl in his voice now, but he suspected the former. Rose looked exhausted.

Weeks with Sally, fighting her influence. Her sway. Just being close to her was enough to twist a man's mind. Miller had felt the effects himself. Though he'd not spent nearly as much time with her as Rose. Or Jonas.

Jonas.

He shuttered to ask. But he needed to know.

Every day since Rose left, Miller had waited, expecting to see Jonas walk in that door. He expected Rose to pry Jonas out of Sally's grip and hide him away from her the way he had done for

Miller. But each day that passed and Jonas didn't arrive, Miller became more and more certain of why.

He hesitated, afraid to ask. "What about Decker?"

Mr. Rose looked at the locket, then to the floor. His expression somber. "I was too late. I tried for days to get close to him, but he never left her side. When I went into her shop, he was... she'd already..." He gestured toward the locket. "He'd already opened it."

Miller's heart sank. He pulled a photograph from his pocket. It was him and Jonas Decker standing in front of the Pub right after Decker opened it. Happy. Smiling. Friends. It was one of the few pictures he had of them together. Decker always did hate having his picture taken.

Jefferson Miller and Jonas Decker had been friends since they were children. They were completely different types of men, from completely different backgrounds, but they never let that stop them. Sure, Decker had his moments of petty jealousy, and Miller wasn't above a jab or two at Decker's expense, but it was never serious. Not until Sally moved in.

The minute she walked up the cobblestone path, it seemed like Decker forgot that they'd ever been friends. Suddenly, things that used to be in jest were meant with seriousness. Harmless teasing between the two of them had turned venomous and angry. Miller had to admit, each time he saw Sally's face, he felt a tinge of it as well. But as soon as he left her sight, the feeling of rivalry faded.

Sally Lockley. That creature. It looked like a woman, but it wasn't. It coiled its barbed vines around Decker and wouldn't release him; poisoning his mind each moment it held him in its grip. Miller was sick with himself that he hadn't noticed it.

"I should have done something."

"There was nothing you could do," Rose said. His voice was soft and sympathetic. "I was lucky to get *you* out of there. Jonas was always a long shot. Man was too close to her. Too tied up in her knots. Every warning about her only spurred him closer. Dug his heels in deeper."

Rose sat down next to him on the sofa. He looked over at the photograph Miller held.

"May I?" Rose held out his hand, and Miller handed him the picture.

Rose looked up at a nearby wall where a framed photo hung. Rose with two other men. The writing below it read, *Misters Cutmore, Portent, and Rose.* Rose gave a sad sigh. "Cutmore was my friend. Wouldn't have even known about Sally or that locket, if he hadn't gotten involved with her. But I couldn't undo what she did to him." He looked at Miller and smiled. "Vengeance is pretty good, though. You think?"

Miller glowered at the locket and nodded. He thought of Sally's screaming, tormented face locked away inside. Rose was right; there was a certain satisfaction to it. "Vengeance'll do."

Rose put a friendly hand on Miller's shoulder and handed the photograph back to him.

Miller looked up at the picture on the wall. "Why isn't Cutmore here?"

Rose smiled and shook his head. "He doesn't understand what Sally is. What she did to him. Even after she sucked the life and youth right out of him. Thinks she poisoned him. That she has some sort of exotic poison hidden away in that locket. And breathing it in aged and disfigured him."

"So he doesn't know the truth about it? Are you ever going to tell him?"

"*Cutmore?*" he scoffed and shook his head. "No. There'd be no getting him to believe in carnivorous jewelry."

Miller let out a small laugh, despite himself. "Carnivorous jewelry... not something you hear every day." He stared at the locket sitting on the table. "It's still dangerous, isn't it?"

"Not a doubt in my mind," Rose answered. "I'm not sure what it can do without her, but I can guarantee you it's trying to figure that out."

Miller shook his head. "We can't let that happen. We have to do something with it, make sure it doesn't end up in the wrong hands."

Rose smiled. "Oh, I have just the place for it. He sat his drink down on the table and gestured for Miller to follow him."

They walked toward a large velvet curtain hanging at the back of the room. Rose pulled back the curtain, revealing a heavy wooden door. Miller had been staying there for weeks and never noticed it there. He followed Rose through the door and into the darkness.

CHAPTER TWENTY
The Dreary Portent

Mr. Rose led Dr. Miller through the dark and into a large room filled with all manner of odd items. Shelves of knick-knacks and baubles. A large frame hung empty on the far wall; it looked as though it had once held a painting, but the current canvas was blank. The sign in front read, *do not touch wet paint.*

Miller furrowed his brow as he read it. "An odd sign to place in front of an empty painting, isn't it?"

"Depends on the time of day," Rose smiled. It was a cryptic tone that Miller had grown to expect from him. Rose quickly grabbed a cloth and tossed it over the frame, hiding it from sight.

Miller walked warily past a shelf of small porcelain dolls. He couldn't be certain, but it felt like they were watching him as he passed. He now had a better view of the room. They'd come in the back way, but they were clearly in a shop. He looked out the window, across the street diagonally he could see his own office, sitting empty on the corner. He hadn't realized how close he was the whole time. It felt like he'd been miles away.

"We're in that little curiosity shop? Next to the bakery?"
Rose nodded.
"I tried to come in here a few times, but it was never open."

"We're not really ready for customers." Rose walked toward a large bookcase filled with leather journals. "Not in this town, at least."

"You have stores in other towns?"

Rose smiled. "We get around."

"So, is this what you do?" Miller asked. "Travel the world rescuing people from monsters?"

Rose laughed and shook his head. "Not exactly. Honestly, I'm not much in the *rescue* business. My line of work is more... *acquisitions*."

"You collect things? Like the locket?"

Rose nodded. "I don't generally get involved anymore than I have to."

"Then why help me? And warn Decker and Gus about Sally?"

"I needed you all to stay away from her so I could do what I came to town for; get the locket. Every time she fed, it meant longer before I could draw her to me."

"So we were in your way?"

Rose shrugged. "Have to stay on schedule," he teased.

"And here I thought we were friends," Miller said with a smirk.

Rose gave Miller a small smile. "It may not be what I usually do, but I am glad I saved you. I like you, Doc. And you *believed me* when I warned you about her, which is rare." He sighed and shook his head. "People never believe."

Rose hung the locket in a velvet display box near the counter. It sat, looking startlingly innocent in its new home. It was unsettling just how normal it would seem to anyone who didn't know what it had done.

Miller looked around the room. Dozens of items lined the shelves. It was only beginning to dawn on him how dangerous this little shop might be. "Are all of these items like that locket?"

"More or less. Some are safe in the right hands, some are dangerous, and some are just... waiting."

"Waiting? Waiting *for what*?"

Rose gave a mischievous shrug. "Suppose we'll find out."

"We?"

"Here's the thing, Doc. Sometimes we come across items that are a bit out of my depth."

Miller furrowed his brow.

Rose reached up and pulled down a black, leather-bound journal from the bookcase. There were dozens of identical ones. Some had names embossed on the covers, but this one's cover was unmarked. Rose sat the book on the counter and motioned for Miller to come closer. The pages inside were filled with notes and drawings. They all seemed medical in nature.

"A surgeon went mad last year, sliced up one of his patients. No history of violence, no sign of illness. Just... snapped."

"And you don't think that's what happened?"

Rose turned the page of the journal, revealing a drawing of a surgical scalpel. "We think this is the item we're looking for. It's made its way into the hands of a few physicians over the years. They lose control of themselves, carve up a patient or a nurse. Then the scalpel vanishes. Turns up a few years later in a different town, then everything starts again with a new doctor. When this last surgeon was arrested, his belongings were likely sold or donated, but I don't know where. I figure the hospital staff would know where it went, but I can't access hospital records."

"Right, you'd have to be on staff at that hospital, or at least be a visiting doctor for that."

"Exactly," Rose smiled. "Don't suppose you'd be interested in taking a trip with me, Doc?"

Miller was only half listening as he looked over the pages of the journal. He was lost in it all, poring over the notes and diagrams. There were newspaper clippings and drawings noting the previous victims' injuries. It was like nothing he'd ever seen. A morbid curiosity overtook him.

"Doc?"

Miller pulled his eyes away from the journal. "How do you think it's happening? The scalpel, I mean. Is it cursed? Is it alive?" He flipped through the pages, looking for more information. "Do the surgeons remain mad after the scalpel is no longer in their possession, or do they return to their senses?"

"I'm not sure. Never been able to investigate much before."

"Look at these diagrams of the wounds. Each victim has the same series of injuries, even though it was different assailants."

Rose examined the drawings. "I hadn't noticed that."

"How did you ever get on in this place without me?" Miller flashed a smirk and a wink toward Rose.

Rose smiled. "That mean you're coming?"

Miller nodded, and Rose seemed pleased.

"Was afraid you were hoping to get back to your life."

Miller looked out the window toward his office. "I'm bored to tears just pacing around this place, but I'm in no hurry to go back home." So much had changed. It didn't even feel like home anymore. He shook his head. "Honestly, I'm not sure if I ever want to go back there."

"Lucky thing you don't have to." Rose said with a sympathetic tone.

Miller watched out the window as a thick fog rolled and billowed through the streets. It enveloped every sign and building until nothing of the town was visible. But it wasn't just the buildings that were stolen; it was the sounds as well. Doorbells, people talking, the gentle chatter of the neighborhood, all disappeared into the dense white fog. And when it rolled away again, and the streets were back in view, Miller found them all quite unfamiliar. They were no longer on his street. They were no longer in his town.

Miller raised a curious eyebrow at Rose, who only smiled.

"Welcome to The Dreary Portent, Doc."

Also by Megon Lashley

The Dreary Portent
The Window In The Painting
The Gold Flower Locket